DOCTOR PROCTOR'S F.A.R.T. POWDER

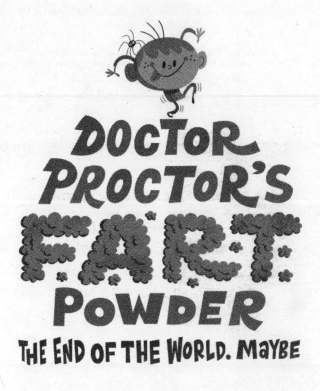

DOCTOR PROCTOR'S F.A.R.T. POWDER

THE END OF THE WORLD. MAYBE

JO NESBØ

SIMON AND SCHUSTER

First published in Great Britain in 2012 by Simon and Schuster UK Ltd
A CBS COMPANY

First published in the USA in 2012 by Aladdin, an imprint of
Simon & Schuster Children's Publishing Division
as *Doctor Proctor's Fart Powder: Who Cut the Cheese?*

Originally published in Norway in 2010 as *Doktor Proktor og verdens undergang. Kanskje.*
by H. Aschehoug & Co.

Text copyright© Jo Nesbø 2010. Published by arrangement with the Salomonsson Agency
English translation copyright © 2012 Tara Chace
Interior illustrations copyright © Mike Lowery 2012

1 3 5 7 9 10 8 6 4 2

Simon & Schuster UK Ltd
1st Floor, 222 Gray's Inn Road
London
WC1X 8HB

Simon & Schuster Australia, Sydney
Simon & Schuster India, New Delhi

A CIP catalogue record for this book is available from the British Library.

PB ISBN: 978-0-85707-389-1
eBook ISBN: 978-0-85707-390-7

Printed and bound by CPI Group (UK) Ltd, Croydon, CR0 4YY

www.simonandschuster.co.uk
www.simonandschuster.com.au

DOCTOR PROCTOR'S F.A.R.T. POWDER

World War
and Hiccups

IT WAS NIGHTTIME in Oslo, Norway, and it was snowing. Big, seemingly innocent snowflakes wafted down from the sky to land on the city's roofs, streets and parks. A weatherperson would surely have explained to you that the snowflakes were just frozen rain, which came from the clouds, but the fact is that no one *really* knows for sure. Snowflakes could, for example, come from the moon, which was visible through gaps in the cloud cover and cast a magical light down over the sleeping city. The snow crystals that hit the asphalt in front of Town Hall melted immediately and ran off as water into the nearest manhole cover, dripping through its openings down into a pipe that led directly into the sewer network that crisscrossed back and forth down there, deep below Oslo.

No one was *really* sure what was actually down there in that sewer world, but if you were so dumb and brave as to climb down there on this December night, remain completely still and hold your breath, you would hear a few strange things. Water dripping, sewage gurgling, rats rustling, a frog croaking. And – if you were really unlucky – the sound of a couple of massive jaws that creaked open into a mouth the size of an inflatable swim ring, the sound of anaconda saliva dripping and then an ear-splitting snap as the orifice slammed shut. After that, it was guaranteed to be complete silence for you, my unlucky friend. But seeing as you weren't so unlucky, you would have heard other sounds on this night, sounds that would amaze you. The sound of a waffle iron closing, of butter sizzling, voices murmuring softly, a waffle iron opening. And then: quiet chewing.

EVENTUALLY THE SNOW stopped falling, the chewing ceased and the people of Oslo started waking up to a new day, heading off through the winter darkness and slush to work and school. And just as Mrs Strobe started telling her students about World War II, a pale winter sun that had overslept once again cautiously peeped over the hilltop.

Lisa was sitting at her desk, looking at the board. Mrs Strobe had written the words WORLD WAR TOO up there. She had misspelled "two." And this was bothering Lisa – who liked things to be spelled correctly – so much that she wasn't quite able to concentrate on Mrs Strobe, who was talking about how the Germans had attacked Norway in 1940 and how a handful of heroes had squared things away with those Germans, so that the Norwegians had won the war and could sing, "Victory is ours, we won the war, victory is ours."

"Well, what was everyone else doing, then, huh?"

"We raise our hands when we want to ask a question, Nilly!" Mrs Strobe said sternly.

"Yes, I bet you do," Nilly said. "But I don't see how that would result in answers that were any better. My method, Mrs Strobe, is just to plunge right in and . . ." The tiny little red-haired and very freckled boy named Nilly raised a tiny little hand up in the air as if he were picking invisible apples. "Boom! Grab hold of the conversation, hang on to it, keep it under my control, give wings to my words and let them fly towards you . . ."

Mrs Strobe bent her head and stared, her eyes

bulging over the tops of her glasses, which slipped yet another inch farther down her long nose. And to her alarm, Lisa saw that Mrs Strobe had raised her hand in preparation for one of her infamous desk slaps. The sound of the flesh on Mrs Strobe's hand striking wood was terrifying. It was said that it had been known to make grown men sob and mothers cry for their mummies. Although, now that Lisa thought about it, Nilly was the one who had told her that; so she wasn't a hundred percent sure that it was a hundred percent true.

"What were the people who weren't heroes doing?" Nilly repeated. "Answer, my dear teacher, whose beauty is exceeded only by your wisdom. Answer and let us drink from the font of your knowledge."

Mrs Strobe lowered her hand and sighed. And Lisa thought she could see the corners of the woman's mouth twitching despite all her strictness. Mrs Strobe was not a lady given to overdoing smiling or any of the other sunnier facial expressions.

"The Norwegians who weren't heroes during the war," Mrs Strobe began. "They . . . uh, rooted."

"Rooted?" Nilly asked.

"They rooted for the heroes. And for the king, who had escaped to London."

"So, they did nothing," Nilly said.

"It's not that simple," Mrs Strobe replied. "Not everyone can be a hero."

"Why not?" Nilly asked.

"Why not what?" Mrs Strobe asked.

"Why can't everyone be a hero?" Nilly asked, flipping his red hair, which because of his stature was only just slightly visible above the edge of his desk.

In the silence that followed, Lisa could hear yelling and hiccuping from the classroom next door to theirs. And she knew it was the new crafts teacher, whose name was Gregory Galvanius but whom they just called Mr Hiccup because he started hiccuping whenever he was feeling stressed out.

"Truls!" Gregory Galvanius screeched in a desperate falsetto. "*Hiccup!* Trym! *Hiccup!*"

Lisa heard the mean laugh of Truls and the almost equally mean laugh of his twin brother Trym, then footsteps running and a door being flung open.

"Not everyone has it in them to be heroes," Mrs Strobe continued. "Most people just want peace and quiet so they can go on about their business without being bothered too much by other people."

By now most of the class had stopped paying attention and were staring out of the windows instead. Because they could see Truls and Trym Thrane running around out there on the snow-covered playground. It was not a pretty sight, because Truls and Trym were two very fat children, and the thighs of their trousers rubbed together as they ran. But the person chasing them wasn't any more elegant. Mr Hiccup was struggling along in the morning sunlight in a bent-over, knock-kneed trot, like a clumsy moose in fuzzy slippers. The reason he was struggling and bent over was that his desk chair appeared to have become stuck to the seat of Mr Hiccup's trousers, and he was awkwardly lugging it around with him.

Mrs Strobe looked out of the window and sighed heavily. "Nilly, I'm afraid some people quite simply are just very normal people without a speck of anything heroic in them."

"What's with that chair?" Nilly asked softly.

"Looks like someone *sewed* it onto his trousers," Lisa said with a yawn. "And uh-oh, he's almost to the icy parts. . . ."

The fuzzy slippers that belonged to Gregory Galvanius, a.k.a. Mr Hiccup, started spinning underneath him. And then he lost his balance and tipped backwards. Right onto his bum. And since his rear end was sewn to the chair, and the chair had wheels, and the wheels were nicely lubricated and the schoolyard sloped gently downward towards Cannon Creek,

Mr Hiccup suddenly found himself an unwilling passenger on a desk chair that was rolling downhill with ever increasing speed.

"Good God!" Mrs Strobe exclaimed in alarm as she discovered her colleague's rapid journey towards the end of the world – or at least the end of school grounds.

For several seconds, it was so quiet that the only thing that could be heard was the rumbling of the chair wheels over the ice, the brushing sound of slippery slippers desperately trying to brake, plus a frantic hiccuping. Then the chair and the crafts teacher hit the snowdrift at the edge of the playground. And the drift sort of exploded with a poof, and the next instant the air was filled with powdery snow. The chair and Gregory Galvanius had disappeared without a trace!

"Man overboard!" bellowed Nilly, who leaped up and hopped from desk to desk over to the door. And everyone else followed, even Mrs Strobe, and as fast as you could count "one, two, three," everyone

was outside, except for Lisa. Lisa was standing by the chalkboard with a piece of chalk in her hand, and with her finger she erased the first *O* in TOO and wrote a *W* in its place: WORLD WAR TWO. There. Then she ran outside too.

OVER BY THE snowdrift, Mrs Strobe and another teacher were already hauling Gregory Galvanius, who was still stuck to his chair, out of the snow.

"Are you okay, Gregory?" Mrs Strobe asked.

"Hiccup!" Gregory said. "I'm blind!"

"No you're not," Mrs Strobe said, using her finger to brush away the snow that was packed inside his glasses. "There."

Galvanius blinked in confusion and then blushed when he saw her. "Oh, hi, Rosemary – I mean, Mrs Strobe! *Hiccup!*"

"What a commotion," Lisa said to Nilly, who had been the first one on the scene, moving so fast he had been coated by the cloud of powdery white snow Galvanius had kicked up. Nilly didn't respond, just stared down at Cannon Creek.

"Is something wrong?" Lisa asked.

"I saw something down there when I got here. The snow cloud covered it."

"Covered what?" Lisa asked.

"That's what I don't know," Nilly said. "Then the snow melted, and it was gone."

Lisa sighed. "Soon we're going to have to do something about your overactive imagination, Nilly. Maybe Doctor Proctor can invent some kind of imagination muffler."

Nilly blinked the snow out of his eyelashes and grabbed her hand. "Come on!" he said.

"Nilly . . . " Lisa protested.

"Come on," Nilly said, zipping up his jacket.

"We're in the middle of a class!" Lisa protested.

But that didn't sway Nilly. He just dove into the

deep snow and was now sliding on his stomach down the steep slope that led to the iced-over creek.

"Nilly!" Lisa cried, wading after him. "We're not allowed to go down to the creek!"

Nilly, who was already back up on his feet again, pointed triumphantly to something in the snow.

"What is it?" Lisa asked, moving closer.

"Tracks," Nilly said. "Footprints."

Lisa looked down at what were, sure enough, deep footprints in the snow. They continued out onto the ice, where there was only a thin layer of snow.

"Someone walked across the creek," Lisa said. "So what?"

"But look at those tracks," Nilly said. "They're not from an animal, right?"

Lisa thought about all the animal tracks they had studied in science classes over the years. Paws, claws, chicken scratch. This didn't look like any of them. So she nodded in agreement.

"And they're not from shoes or boots," Nilly said. "Mysterious . . ."

He started shuffling along, following the tracks out onto the ice.

"Wait!" Lisa cried. "What if the ice isn't . . ."

But Nilly wasn't listening. And once he made it safely to the other side, he turned around and said, "Well, are you coming or what?"

"Just because the ice held for you, it could still be too thin to hold me," Lisa whispered, scared that Mrs Strobe would see them from the playground.

"Huh?" Nilly yelled.

Lisa pointed at the ice.

Nilly responded by pointing at his head. "Use that peanut brain of yours, would you? Look at those tracks! Whatever crossed the creek here is bigger than you and me combined!"

Lisa hated it when Nilly acted like he was smarter than her. So she angrily stomped her feet in the snow a couple of times and thought about what her commandant father – or even worse, her commandant mother – would say when she came home from school with a note from Mrs Strobe. She knew she didn't want that at all. But she walked across the ice anyway, because that's just how it is when you're unlucky enough to happen to be best friends with a guy named Nilly.

THE TRACKS RAN in a big circle through Hazelnut Woods, which was actually just a collection of nice trees, across Hazelnut Bridge, back to the playground, and up the stairs into the gym. Lisa and Nilly opened the door and went in.

"Look," Nilly said, pointing at the wet footprints on the floor. But the footprints got less and less clear as Lisa and Nilly walked down the hallway, through the locker rooms and finally found themselves standing in the empty gym, looking at the last traces of the footprints before they disappeared entirely.

"Their feet must have dried off," Nilly said, sniffing the air.

"What is up with *that*?" Lisa asked, looking at the marching-band banner, which was leaning up against the wall behind the gym mats and the old pommel horse. The gym was where they had band rehearsal. Nilly played the trumpet, and Lisa played clarinet. The banner for their band was blue, and their name was embroidered in yellow: DØLGEN SCHOL MARCHING BAND.

Nilly started walking towards the exit again, and Lisa scurried after him. Because even though she was a sensible, brave girl who did not at all believe in ghosts, monsters or that kind of thing ("Hah! What ten-year-old would believe in that kind of thing," she scoffed), she still didn't want to be left in the gym alone. Because there was something in there that had made the hairs on the back of her neck stand up, something that wasn't right.

Back out in the playground, the headmistress was

standing in front of the snowdrift asking loudly if anyone could tell her who had sewn the seat of Mr Galvanius's trousers to the chair. Nilly and Lisa stood at the top of the stairs by the door to the gym and watched the kids looking around in fear – first at the headmistress, then at Truls and Trym, who were standing shoulder to shoulder with their arms crossed, staring menacingly back at them.

"No one will ever dare to tell on Truls and Trym," Lisa said.

"I guess Mrs Strobe was right," Nilly said. "Most people just want peace and quiet so they can go about their business without being bothered too much by other people."

Right then the bell rang. And Lisa thought this was turning out to be a really strange day.

AND IT GOT even stranger in the middle of their last class. Because that's when Lisa figured out what hadn't been right. The realisation bopped her in the head like one of Truls and Trym's snowballs. The marching-band banner! The banner with the name embroidered in yellow that she had seen hundreds of times: DØLGEN SCHOOL MARCHING BAND. Only the banner they had seen that morning said DØLGEN SCHOL MARCHING BAND. One of the Os was missing. Lisa suddenly felt ice cold. How could that be?

THE BELL HAD rung and Lisa had dragged Nilly back into the empty gym, where they were standing, staring at the old marching-band banner. Nilly spelled his way through the letters with difficulty: "D-Ø-L-G-E-N. S-C-H-O-O-L. M-A-R-C-H-I-N-G. B-A-N-D."

"But there was only one O in the word 'school' this morning!" Lisa said miserably. "Honest!"

Nilly put the tips of the fingers on both hands together and turned to face her. He said, "Hm, maybe

Doctor Proctor can invent some kind of imagination muffler for you, my dear."

"I'm not imagining a thing!" Lisa yelled crossly.

Nilly gave her a friendly pat on the back. "I was just kidding. You know what the difference is between you and me, Lisa?"

"No. Wait, yes. Just about everything."

"The difference, Lisa, is that as your friend, I always believe what you say. Completely."

"That," Lisa said, "is because the difference between you and me is that I always tell the truth."

Nilly studied the banner thoughtfully. "I think it might just be time for us to get some advice from our friends."

"We don't have any *friends*, Nilly. Aside from each other, we only have *one* friend!"

"That sounds like a whole herd of friends if you ask me," Nilly said and started tentatively whistling the trumpet melody from the "Old Ranger's March," the traditional Norwegian military march. And since he was doing that, Lisa couldn't help herself. She joined in, whistling the clarinet part.

And to the tune of the "Old Ranger's March," they marched out of school onto Cannon Avenue, past the red house where Lisa lived, past the yellow one across the street from it where Nilly lived, to the strange, crooked blue house all the way at the end of the street, almost hidden below the snowdrifts, where their only friend lived. They waded through the snow past the leafless pear tree and knocked on the door, since the doorbell was still broken.

"Doctor Proctor!" Nilly yelled. "Open up!"

Balancing Shoes and Moon Chameleons

BUT NO ONE came to open the door at Doctor Proctor's house.

"Where can he be?" Nilly mumbled, peeking in the letter box.

"There," Lisa said.

"Where?" Nilly asked.

"Up there."

Nilly turned and followed Lisa's index finger.

And there, balancing up on the ridgeline of the roof, he saw a tall, thin man wearing a professor's coat and pink earmuffs. The man was taking tiny little steps forwards, walking with his hands out in front of him.

"Doctor Proctor!" Nilly yelled as loud as he could.

"He can't hear you," Lisa said. "He's wearing Double Deaf."

Double Deaf – or Doctor Proctor's Double Deaf Earmuffs – was something the professor had invented to protect people's hearing from another one of his inventions: Doctor Proctor's Fartonaut Powder.

Lisa made a snowball and chucked it. It landed on the roof right in front of the professor, who jumped and started performing an odd-looking dance up there. His arms made a sort of shovelling motion, knocking the pink earmuffs so they covered one of his eyes.

"What are you doing?" Nilly yelled.

"I'm . . . I'm waving my arms around!" the professor yelled, waving his arms even more frantically. "And swaying my upper body. . ." He groaned as his long, thin torso started swaying back and forth. "And losing my balance!" he screamed, and suddenly vanished.

Lisa and Nilly looked at each other in horror. Then they ran around the house.

"Hello?" Lisa yelled.

"Hello?" Nilly yelled.

"Hello, yes," came a dry, hollow response from a hole in the snow with two hands sticking out of it. "And if we're done with the hellos now, could I maybe get a little help over here?"

Lisa and Nilly each grabbed a hand, and for the second time on this odd day, an adult was pulled out of the snow. Although, true enough, most people who knew Doctor Proctor wouldn't exactly call him an adult. Sure, he'd been alive for quite a number of years. But the things he invented were ridiculously fun and, unfortunately, not particularly practical in an adult world. Which is why he was neither rich nor famous. But he was a happy man all the same. He had what he wanted. Every day he got to do what he liked best, namely, invent slightly silly things. He had a garden with a pear tree. And a couple of good friends. And he was engaged to the world's nicest woman, who – as far as he could see through those grimy swim goggles he always wore – was also the most beautiful woman in Oslo, Juliette Margarine. Juliette was currently in Paris but would be joining Doctor Proctor soon.

"Why were you wearing Double Deaf?" Lisa asked as she helped the doctor to his feet.

"My ears were so cold, but I couldn't find my hat," the professor said. "What's up?"

Lisa told him what had happened at school.

"Gregory Galvanius, huh?" Doctor Proctor said, brushing the snow out of his tousled hair. "Quite a creature, that one."

"You know Mr Hiccup?" Nilly asked. "Truls and Trym sewed his trousers to his desk chair in a sort of really ugly cross-stitch. Artistry and craftsmanship are rather elusive skills, aren't they? But I wonder how they did that without him noticing anything."

Doctor Proctor sighed. "I'm sure Gregory probably fell asleep, poor man."

"Teachers don't fall asleep in the middle of their own classes," Lisa said.

"Actually, they do," Doctor Proctor said. "If they're creatures that really should have been hibernating, they do."

"Hmm. Uh, what are those?" Nilly asked, pointing at Doctor Proctor's feet.

"Those," the professor said, looking down at his red and orange boots with blue laces, "are my latest invention: Doctor Proctor's Balancing Shoes. See. . ." He raised one foot and showed them the sole. "It's a pair of old boxing shoes that I installed magnetic tracks in, so you can balance on anything. You just flip on this switch here."

A normal knob from a stove was attached to the boot's instep. Lisa read the settings:

TIGHT LINE

SLACK LINE

FENCE

BRIDGE

ROOF

"Cool!" Nilly exclaimed. "Can I try?"

"Not yet, my dear Nilly. It needs a little perfecting before it'll be . . . uh, perfect."

"Well, if that's the case, why were *you* just wearing them up on the roof?" Nilly asked, a little poutily. When Nilly tested one of Doctor Proctor's inventions, the ones he liked best were the ones that weren't quite perfect yet.

"I was adjusting the antenna," Doctor Proctor said, pointing up at his roof where the outlines of an enormous television antenna were clearly visible in straight, black lines silhouetted against the pale winter sky. "I hardly get a single TV channel these days."

Lisa groaned. "But my dear professor! Don't you know that the TV signals are all digital now? None of those old antennas work anymore."

Doctor Proctor raised an eyebrow and looked at Lisa, then up at the antenna on his roof, and then at his watch. "Well, the clock's ticking. What's up?"

"Excuse me?" Lisa said.

"What's up?" Doctor Proctor repeated.

"I saw something that disappeared when the snow melted," Nilly said.

"That's what snow does when it melts," Doctor Proctor said with a yawn. "What else is going on?"

"The school banner was missing an *O*," Lisa said.

"Sounds like the end of the world is coming," Doctor

Proctor said, starting to trudge through the snow towards his front door.

"Do you have any advice about what we should do?" Lisa asked.

"Of course," said Proctor.

"And what would that be?" Lisa prompted.

"What we always do. We'll make jelly."

"WELL," DOCTOR PROCTOR said after the three of them had finished off a five-foot-long jelly at the professor's kitchen table. On the counter sat the model helicopter he had used to whip the cream to put on top, the toaster he had used to do a quick dry on his mittens and socks, and a pot for cooking fish soup that he had made a big hole in the bottom of because he couldn't stand fish soup.

"So, you saw something," Doctor Proctor said.

"Yup," Nilly said, and burped loudly. "Excuse me."

"Of course. What did you see?"

"Hard to say. It was sort of dusted with a little flurry of snow after Gregory Galvanius's collision. I could see its silhouette. But then the snow melted, and whatever was underneath was invisible."

"Human or animal?"

"Don't know. The tracks didn't look like any animal tracks I've seen. Or like any person who was barefoot or wearing shoes or boots. It was like it was wearing . . ." Nilly squeezed his eyes shut and looked like he was concentrating rather hard on what it might have been wearing.

"Hm," said Doctor Proctor. "And that banner that was missing the *O* in 'school.' But then when you went back, the *O* was there again?"

Lisa nodded.

Doctor Proctor rubbed his chin.

"Socks!" Nilly yelled.

Lisa and Doctor Proctor looked at him.

"They were sock footprints," Nilly said. "You know

like if you get soaked and come home and take off your shoes and walk around in just your wet socks on the floor."

"Sock thief," whispered Proctor, as if to himself. "Speech impediment. Moonka—" Then it was as if he realised that Nilly and Lisa were sitting there and he suddenly stopped talking.

"Sock thief?" Lisa and Nilly asked in unison.

"Speech impediment!" Proctor said. "I mean . . . my speech was impeded . . . I misspoke." He pointed out of the window: "Would you look at that! Look, it started snowing!"

They glanced out, and sure enough a few tiny grains of snow were falling. But it was Norway, and it snowed a lot there.

Lisa looked at Doctor Proctor and asked, "What's a sock thie—"

"Anyway, I'm working on a new invention," Proctor said, interrupting her before she had a chance to finish.

"It's a mutant hybrid between a Christmas tree and a normal pine tree that makes it so the trees can grow tinsel, paper chains and lights. All you have to do is chop it down and set it up in your living room already decorated. What do you think?"

Nilly shook his head and said, "Bad idea. Half the fun is in decorating the tree yourself."

"Really?" Doctor Proctor asked.

"Yup," Nilly said, scraping his jelly plate. "Couldn't you invent something that would make the Dølgen School Marching Band sound good instead?"

"*That* I think is impossible," Doctor Proctor said. "But what about gingerbread-flavoured jelly?"

"You're onto something there!" Nilly cried, glancing at the last little bit of jelly left in the serving dish. "If no one else is having any more, then maybe I could . . ."

"Doctor Proctor," Lisa said, "what were you saying about a sock thief?

"Never heard of such a thing," Proctor said. "And neither have you two."

Lisa looked over at Nilly. His cheeks were puffed up like two balloons and the jelly plate was empty.

"Well, well, would you look at the time," Doctor Proctor said, and then yawned, loudly and obviously.

"DON'T YOU THINK Doctor Proctor was acting a little weird tonight?" Lisa asked as they stood on his front porch.

"Nah," said Nilly, who then burped loudly and smiled contentedly.

"Exactly," Lisa said, rolling her eyes.

After Lisa got home, ate dinner, did her home-work and practised her clarinet, her mother called from down in the living room that she thought it was time for Lisa to go to bed. And, actually, Lisa agreed with her. After she brushed her teeth, she went down to the living room to say goodnight. Her parents were sitting there watching TV. A bunch of men and women were singing at the top of their lungs, white capes swaying like curtains in a summer breeze. And Lisa realised she longed for spring.

"What are you watching?" Lisa asked.

"What are we *watching*?" her commandant father gasped. "This is the NoroVision Choral Throwdown. The winning chorus gets twenty thousand krone and fifty øre. Plus their own TV show. Plus an all-expenses-paid camping trip to Denmark."

"Plus free haircuts for six months in the towns of Moss or Voss, or any other rhyming town," Lisa's mother said. "Plus—"

"Who's that singing?" Lisa interrupted.

"That's Hallvard Tenorsen's chorus," her father muttered.

"Who's Hallvard Tenorsen?" Lisa asked.

"Who's Hallvard Tenorsen?" her mother repeated, shocked. "Honestly, Lisa, you ought to keep up with the tabloids a little more. Hallvard Tenorsen's that singing chiropractor from Jönköping, Sweden. Haven't you heard of him, Lisa? The cutest choral conductor south of the North Pole. Just look! See how cute he is? Odd that he isn't married."

"Not odd that he isn't married," Lisa's father chuckled.

Lisa looked at the wide-open mouths of the singing, smiling chorus members, then she left.

Once Lisa was in bed, she turned off her reading light, turned on her flashlight and shone it on a window in the yellow house across the street. And as usual the light over there turned on and a couple of itty-bitty fingers started putting on a shadow play. Tonight the performance seemed to be about a hiccuping man rolling away and crashing into something. And a woman with a long nose helping him up. The man looked like he was trying to kiss her, but she brushed him aside. Lisa laughed out loud. And totally forgot that she had forgotten what she had forgotten. So when the performance was over, Lisa fell into her normally sound sleep abnormally quickly. And she didn't notice that it had stopped snowing or that a strange murmuring sound had started rising from the manhole cover out on Cannon Avenue. The murmuring rose up towards the moon, which twinkled sleepily down on Oslo as it hummed a song.

Seven-Legged Spiders
and Apollo II

AT SCHOOL THE next day everyone was talking
about the choral competition and who had given the
best performance.

Some said, "Hallvard Tenorsen's chorus."

Others said, "The Hallvard Tenorsen Chorus."

While a number of other others said just, "Hallvard Tenorsen."

The final, deciding round of the NoroVision Choral Throwdown was tonight. Of course everyone would be watching, and the person they would be paying most attention to was Hallvard Tenorsen.

During lunch break, the girls sat on the bench in the hallway eating from their lunchboxes and talking about Tenorsen's soft hair, that practically covered those gentle, blue eyes. And those perfect teeth, standing to attention like a whitewashed picket fence in his mouth.

"Seriously," said Beatrize, who wasn't just the cutest girl in their class, but was also the best at maths, PE, Chinese jump rope and pretty much everything else that mattered at their school. "I think we ought to start our own chorus and enter the competition next year."

And as usual when Beatrize expressed an opinion,

the other girls nodded in agreement. Everyone aside from Lisa, who had just barely and politely managed to eke out a tiny bit of space at the very end of the bench.

Beatrize flipped her long, blonde hair and studied her freshly painted nails: "I'm just dead sure we could win, you know. I mean, *look* at us, you know? We so totally *ooze* charm and inner beauty and all that stuff."

Lisa rolled her eyes, but none of the other girls noticed. And if they had, they would hardly have cared.

"But, like, how can we just *start* a chorus, huh, Beatrize?" one of the girls asked.

"Easy," Beatrize said, checking her hair for split ends. "All we need is, like, a conductor."

"But how do we just, you know, *get* one of those, huh?"

Someone up above them exclaimed: "A conductor?"

And just then something came plopping down and landed on the floor right in front of them with the slap of two tiny shoe soles, children's size 11. His eyes shone among the freckles. On his little head he was wearing an enormous orange knit hat with a pom-pom on top, askew. "Super. I'll take the job," Nilly said.

"Like, where did *you* come from?" Beatrize asked.

"That little shelf up there where people put their hats," he answered, crumpling the paper bag his lunch had been in and tossing it in a perfect arc up and over into the bin can next to Lisa. "When do I start?"

Beatrize rolled her eyes. "What, like we're going to have some red-haired dwarf as our conductor?"

The other girls snickered.

"Like that would get us a lot of votes," one of them whispered.

"A few people might find it funny," whispered another.

"Not very many. He's hardly more than a dust bunny," Beatrize said.

"Well, my offer expires in exactly five seconds," Nilly said. "Four, three . . . so, what do you say?"

And the answer actually sounded like it came from a chorus: "NOOOO!!!"

"No, well then," Nilly said. "Don't come to school complaining and saying you never got your chance when we win next year."

"We?" Beatrize asked.

"Yup," Nilly said.

"Who's we?"

"Lisa singing soprano and me as tenor."

The girls laughed hysterically, but Lisa looked hurt. "Nilly . . ." she began.

"Well, do you guys have a name then?" Beatrize scoffed.

"Of course," Nilly said, writing the letters in the air with his index finger as he pronounced the name slowly and exaggeratedly: "Nilly's Very Harmonic and Very Mixed Chorus."

"Ha, ha," Beatrize laughed disdainfully. "You guys have a, like, chorus with just two people in it? Hallvard

Tenorsen must have, like, at least thirty in his."

"Who said just two?" Nilly asked. "Obviously there's more of us."

"Like, who? I mean, like totally, who?" Beatrize scoffed.

"Well, there's Doctor Proctor singing baritone," Nilly said, squeezing his eyebrows together as he counted on his fingers, as if it were hard to remember everyone. "And . . . singing contralto we have his fiancée, Juliette Margarine. Well, if she were here. And then of course there's the castrato; we've got Perry, who sings that part."

"Well, like, who's Perry?"

"He's a seven-legged Peruvian sucking spider. He can sing notes so high that an unmusical human ear can't even hear them. It's delightful."

"Bah," Beatrize said. "You're just, like, making all this stuff up as usual, Nilly. Everyone knows there's no such thing as a seven-legged Peru . . . Peru . . ."

"Peruvian sucking spider," Lisa finished her sentence for her and sighed. This was all actually even more embarrassing than usual.

"There isn't?" Nilly said. "Well, then, say hello to . . ." He whipped off his orange hat. ". . . Perry!"

The girls shrieked, some of them so loudly that they dropped their sandwiches on the floor. Because there, actually sitting on top of Nilly's head, was a black, bow-legged spider. True, it didn't look particularly Peruvian, eager to suck or enthusiastic about singing, but it was a spider. And if you counted, sure enough, it did have seven legs. But since it wasn't an especially big or an especially hairy spider, the girls quickly recovered their senses.

"But c-c-can it, you know, *sing*?" Beatrize scoffed.

"Of course," Nilly said. "Sing something popular, Perry. Yeah, that one! Good pick, Perry!"

The girls stared with their mouths agape at Nilly and the spider, which was standing motionless and bowlegged on top of that fire-engine-red mane of hair of his.

"Isn't it wonderful?" cried Nilly, who had closed his eyes and was moving his head from side to side, enraptured, as he sang along: "Hallelujah, Hallelujah . . ."

"Seriously," Beatrize said. "I totally only hear Nilly."

"Of course," sighed Lisa. "As he said, sucking spiders sing so high that unmusical ears can't hear it."

Beatrize stared at Lisa with her mouth hanging

open. Because music was something that mattered at their school, and here was Lisa practically just saying it out loud – that she, Beatrize, was unmusical!

"Hallelujah, hallelujah," Lisa sang, and started moving her head in time with Nilly's.

"Seriously," Beatrize scoffed, standing up. "Let's go, chorus girls."

And with that they turned their noses up in the air and marched past Lisa and Nilly and Perry out onto the playground.

"Ugh," Lisa said. "*Those* were the girls I wanted to be friends with. And *that* was the chorus I wanted to be in. Ugh. And I had finally got myself a spot on their bench."

"Well, there's more room here now," Nilly said, taking a seat next to her. "And who actually wants to sing in a chorus when they can play in a marching band?"

And when Lisa thought about it, she realised he might be right.

"THAT SURE IS a nice-looking spider."

The voice made Nilly and Lisa jump. Because they hadn't heard anyone approaching. Over them stood the bent form of crafts teacher Gregory Galvanius, who was staring at them – or more accurately at Nilly – with what could almost be interpreted as greedy eyes.

"Mr Hiccup," slipped out of Nilly's mouth.

"Mr Hiccup?" Galvanius asked as his eyelids slid up and down over his slightly bulging eyes, which were trained on Perry. "Is that what you call this fine-looking specimen?"

"Oh, him?" Nilly said. "His friends just call him Perry. Do you like spiders, Mr Galvanius?"

"Very much," Mr Galvanius said, and a long tongue slipped out of his mouth and licked all the way around. "Insects in general, you could say."

"You don't say," Nilly said. "This is a seven-legged—"

"Peruvian sucking spider," Galvanius said. "And a really nice-looking one, too." A thin river of drool had started flowing out of one of the corners of his mouth.

Nilly picked up his orange hat and placed it carefully back onto his head, over Perry.

"Cold," Nilly said by way of an explanation. "Perry's legs get cold so easily. And when you have seven legs that can get cold, well, that's a lot of . . . uh, shivering. Huh?"

Lisa realised that she was standing there staring at Mr Galvanius's shoes. They looked new. Brand-new. Abnormally new, actually. Yes, now that she thought about it, she'd never seen such new shoes.

"What's going on here?" they heard a voice say.

It was Mrs Strobe. Mr Galvanius hiccuped loudly and blushed.

"Shouldn't you be on your way to class right now?" she asked.

"B-but the bell hasn't even rung yet," Lisa said.

And right then the school bell started ringing – as if it were under Mrs Strobe's command. Shrill and buzzing, like a bumblebee trapped in a glass jar.

Nilly and Lisa leaped up and ran to class. And behind them they heard Mrs Strobe's authoritative voice say, "Shouldn't you also be on your way, Gregory?"

"Of course, Mrs Strobe."

And with that, Mr Galvanius bounded away in long, odd hops.

And once Lisa and Nilly were back in the classroom and class had started, Lisa saw Beatrize and the other girls put their heads together, snicker and send malicious looks in her and Nilly's direction. And Lisa thought Nilly was right. Who wanted to sing in a chorus when you could play in a marching band? And there was band practice tonight.

Chorus and Marching Band

ALL OF NORWAY, with a few exceptions, was glued to a TV screen when Nømsk Ull, host of the NoroVision Choral Throwdown, yelled into the camera that it was time for the finale and that the first chorus to face the music would be . . .

Nømsk Ull went up into a falsetto as he flung out his arm towards the stage: ". . . Hallvard Tenorsen and his chorus, Fuhhhhhni Voisis!"

And there they stood in stylish tight black shirts: Funny Voices. And in front of them, in an even more stylish, tighter and blacker shirt: Hallvard Tenorsen himself. He smiled broadly, raised both hands, pinched his thumb and index fingers together as if they were holding something dirty and made a few weird jerks with his head, as if he were experiencing an electric shock. And then his chorus chimed in, singing a BABA song in the thickest Norwegian accents you can imagine:

Hunney, hunney, hunney

Yur so funney

Eets a crazy world!

On the third verse, Tenorsen turned around and smiled into the camera, as if the viewers out there, in those many thousands of Norwegian homes, were supposed to be singing the song as well.

And, sure enough, they were. Norwegians were sitting in their living rooms with their coffee cups or their water bottles or their dummies, singing along about how boring it was to work and how much more fun it would be to be rich.

And once Tenorsen and his chorus had finished, Nømsk Ull came back on-screen and yelled, "Wonderful! If you want to vote for Fuhni Voisis, just call the number you see on the screen!"

And in living rooms across Norway, from the north to the south, people lunged for their phones and voted. And while the other choruses sang and did their best, people munched on potato chips, popcorn, pretzels, pork rinds and other things that start with *P* as they discussed the fabulous Hallvard Tenorsen.

In a hair salon, a stylist giggled and said, "I think

I'd like to have myself a little chiropractic session with that Tenorsen."

In a diner, a long-haul trucker grumbled, "I've heard he can beat three grown men at arm wrestling while simultaneously fixing a flat tyre, playing the ukulele and doing the dishes."

And in an old folks' home, the oldest man there said in a quavering voice: "It said in the paper that he's kissed six hundred and sixty-two girls and women. Plus a few men who looked like women. And one woman he thought was a man who thought he was a woman."

Once all the choruses were done, and it was one minute to seven, Nømsk Ull's face once again filled the screen. "Just keep voting, people. All our lines will be open until eight o'clock Central European Time. That's when this will all be decided and a winner will be announced for the NoroVision Choral . . ." He gestured to the audience so that everyone yelled in unison with him: ". . . Throwdown!"

AT EXACTLY SEVEN o'clock, Mr Madsen adjusted his aviator glasses, cleared his throat and raised his baton. In the gym in front of him sat the boys, girls, trumpets, clarinets, snare drums, Frenchhorns, saxophones, bass drum and tuba, which, all together, comprised the Dølgen School Marching Band. That summer the band had received special recognition at the marching-band competition held in Lillehammer. The judges said it was absolutely the worst marching band they had ever heard and that – with the exception of a couple of talented members, most notably the itty-bitty little red-haired boy on the trumpet – it was a downright impressive assembly of musically ungifted kids that only a real enthusiast could manage to direct for very long. And then they had awarded Mr Madsen his prize, a pair of real leather German earmuffs. Mr Madsen had thrown the earmuffs away, added one extra practice session per week, and now here he stood, counting into the beginning of "Very Old Ranger's March," the one that was composed after the "Old Ranger's March," but before the "New Ranger's March." He wasn't counting up, but down, as if he were standing in front of a bomb that was about to go off: "Four, three, two . . ."

He muttered one final, silent prayer and steeled himself before shouting "One!" and letting his baton fall.

Three minutes later he drew an X in the air with his baton. That meant that the "Very Old Ranger's March" was over. And apart from a belated bleat from a saxophone, they all actually finished more or less at the same time.

"Hm," Mr Madsen said, once silence had settled over the room. He tried to come up with the analogy that would best describe what he had just heard. Because it wasn't *so* awful. Of course there had been a few wayward noises: a nervous clarinet that squeaked, switching into a higher register; a couple of slightly off notes from the French horns; a bass drum beat that was a little off the mark; and something that might have just been a fart from one of the wind players who was straining a little too hard. But by and large, good. Very good, even.

Mr Madsen cleared his throat while the band watched him with anxious eyes.

"Well, that wasn't *that* bad."

Because it was a fact that the Dølgen School Marching Band had made great progress since their disastrous showing at Lillehammer that summer. Mr Madsen glimpsed – for the first time in his life as a band conductor – a bit of hope. Which caused him to feel something he had otherwise never felt before: He was touched. Yes, he was a little moist there behind his sunglasses. He adjusted the glasses to make sure that no one could tell.

"One more time," he said, feeling like he should have cleared his throat first.

And the Dølgen School Marching Band played again. And again. And it just kept sounding better and better.

"We'll just take it from the top one more time before we call it a night," Mr Madsen said.

He raised his baton but then lowered it again before he had started the countdown.

"Where are you going, Truls and Trym?"

Truls and Trym had put away their snare drums, zipped up the zippers of their identical thick jackets, which made them both look like stacks of car tyres and were now on their way out of the door.

"Home to vote for Tenorsen," Truls said. "The voting ends in half an hour."

"But rehearsal isn't over yet," Mr Madsen said.

"We don't care," Truls said. "We quit."

"Q-q-quit?" Mr Madsen adjusted his glasses a couple of times, but there was nothing wrong with his vision and he had not misheard them. Those two bums were actually planning to quit his band!

"But you can't quit now!" Lisa yelled. "Not now that we're finally starting to sound like a proper band."

"Oh, shut up, Flatu-Lisa," said Truls. "This band sucks."

"Sucks massively," Trym said, opening the door.

"Wait!" Mr Madsen yelled. "What are you boys going to do instead of band?"

"We're going to join the chorus."

"The chorus?" Mr Madsen didn't believe his own finely tuned ears. "Who wants to join a *chorus* when you can play in a band?"

"Us," Truls said. "And them."

He pointed at Beatrize and two of her friends, who were also putting away their instruments.

"And them," Trym said, pointing at all three of the French-horn players, who were all clicking shut the latches on their French-horn cases.

"What's going on here?" Mr Madsen yelled, banging

his baton against the edge of his music stand. But it didn't do any good. Quite the contrary – more and more of the kids started putting away their instruments.

"This is mutiny!" screamed Nilly, jumping up onto his chair.

But no one seemed to hear him. They were marching out of the gym, and as Beatrize, the last of them, left, she turned and stuck her tongue out at Nilly and slammed the door behind her with a bang.

Once silence had again settled over the gym, Lisa looked around. Aside from herself, Nilly and Mr Madsen, the only one left was Janne, the tuba player, a girl who never talked to anyone and wore patches over both eyeglass lenses because she always went snow-blind in January. And this year was no exception.

Mr Madsen stood there before them with his arms dangling and his bottom lip quivering. He stood there like that for a long time, totally motionless, until

his lower lip had finally stopped trembling. Then he adjusted his glasses, raised his baton and directed his gaze at the three remaining musicians.

"Ready for the 'Very Old Ranger's March'? Four, three, two, one . . ."

WHEN LISA GOT home, she untied her boots and put them in the coat cupboard.

She went into the living room. From behind her parents' armchairs, she saw the TV, where Tenorsen was standing with his arms full of flowers, beaming and smiling at everyone.

"Hey, how's it going?" Lisa asked.

"Tenorsen and Funny Voices just won!" her father laughed gleefully. "Aren't you thrilled?"

"Hi, honey," her mum said without turning around. "You're dinner's on a plate in the fridge."

"Everyone in the band quit to go sing in a chorus, and . . ." Lisa began.

"Shh!" her mum hushed. "Tenorsen is going to conduct again." She and Lisa's father leaned forwards in their chairs.

Lisa sighed and went to the kitchen, where she helped herself to the two bagels already spread with cream cheese. From the living room she heard her parents singing along to a pop song: *"Love. The most beautiful word in the world . . ."*

After Lisa drank her milk and brushed her teeth, she went back in to her parents. The NoroVision Choral Throwdown was over, and a newscaster on TV was reporting that Hallvard Tenorsen wanted to address the nation in a long victory speech following the news.

"Goodnight," Lisa said, giving her mother and father a hug.

"Oh, I forgot to mention," her mother said, "that at the parent-teasher meeting yesterday Mrs Strobe said you would do well to raise your hand a little more in class, since it turns out you always know the right answer."

"Great," Lisa said, not up to explaining that Nilly had usually answered before she could get her hand up in the air. And that his answers generally had very little to do with the questions.

"Oh, and vee met your new arts and crafts teasher," her father said. "Mr Galvanius, isn't it?"

"I thought he was almost a little creepy," her mother said with a shudder. "You know, his hand felt all slimy when vee shook hands with him? Weird fingers, too, looked like they were webbed or something."

Then Lisa's commandant father laughed so his large commandant belly shook. "Ho, ho. Now you're exaggerating, honey. Isn't she, Lisa?"

"Hm," said Lisa, who hadn't heard the question because the newscaster on TV had just caught her attention with a little news item. The bulletin was so small you could easily have failed to notice it, squeezed in as it was between a big earthquake that was comfortably far away and the weather. The news item was just a single sentence, actually. Still, it made the hairs on the back of her neck stand up. Just like when she had been standing in the gym looking at the band banner.

"Sleep well, darling," her father said, kissing Lisa on the forehead.

But when Lisa was in bed trying to fall to sleep, that one sentence kept running through her head. The bit of news was so small that the newscaster had read it with a little smile: "The police are receiving a dramatic increase in reports of missing socks."

Ice Snowballs and Brain Sucking

WHEN NILLY WOKE up the next morning, he could tell something was different. He didn't know what, because pretty much everything was the same as ever. For example, Eva, his big sister, locked the bathroom door and told him to scram and quit bugging her while she made herself beautiful.

"While you pop your zits, you mean?" Nilly asked from the hallway.

"Die, you pathetic little carrot-topped chrimp!" she screamed. "I'm really not in any hurry, you know."

Nilly went down to the kitchen. There he buttered four slices of bread: He ate one, and he wrapped two in wax paper to take to school for lunch. He put the last one on a plate and carried it up to his mother's bedroom along with a glass of orange juice and the morning paper. He set everything down on her bedside table and carefully shook her: "Wake up, O mother of all mothers. It's a beautiful day out there."

She rolled over in bed, stared at him with suspicion in her bloodshot eyes and smacked her lips twice before snorting, "You're lying, the way you usually do, Nilly."

"It's going to be minus eight degrees today and sunny," Nilly read from the paper.

"Shut up and read me the headlines," his mother

said, closing her eyes and rolling back over to face the wall again.

"Hallvard Tenorsen Wins!" Nilly read. "In his victory interview, Tenorsen said that Norway is being mismanaged, that nothing works, that the king and the prime minister are incompetent and that the proud people of Norway ought to elect a leader who knows how things ought to be done as soon as possible. Someone who knows how to get people to work together. Just like the members of a chorus."

"Hm. Any other news?"

"Let's see . . ." Nilly said, squinting to read the tiny headline below the enormous picture of Hallvard Tenorsen. "Apparently there was a big earthquake somewhere."

"Where?" Nilly's sister shrieked from the bathroom.

Nilly squinted at the letters: "Impossible to say."

"Boring," his mother said. "Read me more about Tenorsen."

"Tenorsen said time is of the essence," Nilly read. "'I'm willing to accept the job of steering Norway out of this mess if the people will have me,' Tenorsen volunteered in his televised interview."

Nilly laughed out loud.

"What are you laughing at, you nincompoop!" screamed his sister, who had emerged from the bathroom and was standing in the doorway with small, angry red craters all over her face.

"Tenorsen," Nilly said. "The guy thinks he should be put in charge of the Norwegian government. Can you imagine?!" Nilly wrote in the air, as if he were writing a newspaper headline: "Singing Swedish Chiropractor Takes Charge of Norway."

Nilly laughed so hard he started hiccuping, but stopped when he noticed his mother and Eva staring at him.

"Who are vee going to trust if not Tenorsen?" his mother asked coolly. "You?"

Eva laughed out loud at their mother's joke, and their mother laughed louder because Eva had laughed at her joke, and Eva laughed even louder because her mother was laughing because she was laughing. Nilly looked at the time, set down the paper and went to get his backpack. His mother called after him: "Don't forget to stop by the shop on your way home! We're out of milk and bread, and could you pick up some sheddar sheese."

NILLY WAITED OUTSIDE Lisa's gate as usual until she came out wearing her backpack. And as usual they didn't say a word, just started walking down Cannon Avenue the way they usually did.

"Everything is normal," Lisa said as they approached Truls and Trym's house. "And yet, it's as if . . . as if . . ."

"As if something is very abnormal?" Nilly said. "You feel like that too?"

"My mum and dad – they kind of didn't seem normal."

"Same here," Nilly said. "Although, of course, it's

normal for my sister and my mother to be abnormal."

"And almost our whole band quit just all of a sudden like that. Do you think *that's* normal?"

"No, that is absolutely, unusually abnormal. Eerily abnormal, actually."

"But everything at the Thrane house is normal, anyway," Lisa said, nodding at the fence surrounding the ostentatious home in front of them.

And sure enough: Truls and Trym Thrane were hunkered down in their snow fort behind their fence, watching Nilly and Lisa with evil sneers of anticipation, their snowballs at the ready. Lisa and Nilly usually got a few snowballs lobbed at them as they ran by, but they almost always managed to duck out of the way of the feeble throws, because Truls and Trym had got so fat in the last year that they couldn't swing their arms that well anymore.

But Lisa quickly realised that they weren't going to escape so easily today.

The twins had hopped the fence and were now blocking the pavement. Each twin was holding an enormous snowball. And Lisa saw the first rays of the day's sunlight sparkling off their surfaces and realised that Truls and Trym had poured water on them. Ice-covered snowballs.

Nilly said under his breath: "Don't worry, Lisa. Let me take care of this."

Lisa looked down at her itty-bitty friend. He could be irritating, annoying and run roughshod over the truth. But she didn't know anyone braver. Sometimes he was so brave you had to wonder if he wasn't actually a little dumb.

"Good morning, Captain Thrane and Captain Thrane!" Nilly proclaimed with a radiant smile. "Because those *are* captains' hats you're wearing on your heads, right?"

"Chorus uniform hats," the twins said in unison, looking rather proud. The hats were white with black glossy visors and tassels dangling by cords from the middle.

"Chorus?" Nilly asked. "So you guys don't just play

drums, you sing, too? Who would've thought so much talent could fit into such small bodies."

Truls and Trym stared at Nilly with their mouths hanging open, their breath billowing out as if from two stove chimneys.

"He's just trying to fast-talk us," Trym whispered to his brother. "Him being nice to us."

"But . . ." Truls whispered. "I *believe* him, because he's saying we're good drummers, right?"

"That's because you've been fast-talked," Trym whispered.

"I've been fast-talked," Truls nodded.

"Let's crush him now," Trym whispered. "Crush his head!"

"Yeah, crush that irritating head," Truls said, raising his hand and the clump of ice in it.

"Let me make that head crushing a little easier for you, my dear Thrane brothers," Nilly said, pulling off his orange hat.

"Ha!" the twins laughed, bending their arms back as far as they were physically able.

"What's that on his head?" Trym asked.

"It's an animal," Truls said.

"I can see that, but what kind of animal?"

"A small animal."

"Maybe it's a flea?"

"Yeah," Trym laughed. "The gnome has fleas! Crush him!"

"Have at it," said Nilly, who stood there without moving and smiled. "But as a neighbour I feel I ought to warn you about the consequences of throwing an ice snowball at a seven-legged Peruvian sucking spider."

"Head crushing!" Truls yelled.

"Wait!" Trym said. "What kind of con . . . congo . . . conto . . . quences?"

"Well," Nilly said. "Since it's Peruvian, this sucking spider grew up in the snow-covered Andes Mountains and is quite used to snowballs since snowballs are a very common part of everyday life in the Andes. There are fierce snowball wars up there all the time between rival Inca tribes. Everyone throws snowballs in Peru. Even the llamas. They eat snow and spit it out again as snowballs with spit and snot and whatever else on it. But Perry can take it all. Although, there's taking it and then there's taking it. I mean, if he gets hit, it makes him mad. Very mad. And his revenge is grisly . . ."

"Yeah!" exclaimed Lisa, who was surprised to hear her own voice. But continued, "Enraged, the spider will leap onto the snowball thrower's head faster than you can blink, and slip into the thrower's ear."

"His ear?" Truls asked.

"And he just follows the ear canal inward," Nilly said.

"Ew!" said Trym.

Just the idea made Truls itch, and he tried to stick a finger into his ear to scratch, but forgot he was wearing mittens.

"And when it gets to your brain," Lisa said, "it starts sucking."

"Sucking?!" the twins cried in unison.

"Of course. That's why it's called a sucking spider," Lisa said. "It sucks up . . ." She lowered her voice. Truls and Trym couldn't help but lean in closer to hear her. ". . . your whole brain." And then suddenly she made a loud slurping sound and the twins jumped back in fear.

"Everything you remember about multiplication tables and the countries in Europe and everything else you ever learned in school disappears first," Lisa said. When this didn't seem to alarm them, she continued. "Then you'll forget how to play the national anthem, all your friends' names, how to get home and finally your own names."

But this just made Trym yawn.

"Then . . . then . . ." Lisa said, trying to come up with something else, but drawing a blank.

Truls raised the hand that was holding the clump of ice.

"Then you'll forget to eat," Nilly said. "Pizza, chips, chocolate bars, you won't care about them. You'll be as thin as a string bean and then you'll die of hunger."

Truls and Trym stared at Nilly, their terrified eyes bulging wide.

"He's doing it again," Truls gasped. "He's fast-talking us!"

"Nonsense," Trym said, stretched his hand out to Nilly's head, pulled it back and opened his mitten. There in his palm sat Perry.

"Ha, ha!" Trym laughed triumphantly. "I took it! It's just a totally normal everyday spider!"

"Break off one of its legs!" Truls yelled, jumping up and down. "No, break off *three* legs! Then it'll be a three-legged Peruvish . . . Peruvic . . . Pe . . . sucking spider!"

"Four-legged," Lisa said with a sigh.

"Huh?"

She rolled her eyes. "Seven minus three is four."

"Shut up!" Truls said. "We'll just break off one more."

"I wouldn't do that if I were you," Nilly said.

The twins turned to look at him.

"Everyone knows that the three-legged Peruvian sucking spider is three times more dangerous than the seven-legged variety."

The twins stared at the spider.

"You do it," said Trym, passing the mitten with the spider on it to Truls.

"Me?" Truls asked, pulling back. "You do it!"

"No, you!" Trym said, waving the mitten around.

"You!"

"I'll do it," Nilly said, grabbing the mitten. He carefully picked Perry up and put him back on his head. Then he put on his orange hat and handed the mitten back to Trym.

"But not until later, after I get back home," Nilly said. "Spider leg operations like that have to be done under controlled conditions with cauterisation equipment, anesthesia and under adult supervision. Okay?"

"Okay," Trym said submissively.

"Okay then," Truls said.

"Have an enlightening day," Nilly said.

And with that he and Lisa rushed off to school.

"I didn't know you had that in you," Nilly said once they were out of earshot.

"Had what in me?" Lisa asked.

"That stuff about forgetting your multiplication tables and the national anthem. You're worse about making stuff up than I am."

"No one is worse than you, Nilly."

"Even I wouldn't have come up with . . ." And he repeated the loud, sucking, slurping sound Lisa had made for the twins.

And that made them both laugh until they were

jabbing their fingers into each other jokingly and practically collapsing onto the ice.

And they walked the rest of the way like that, bonking into each other and laughing and making slurping sounds.

IT WASN'T UNTIL well into their first class, when Mrs Strobe was giving the class an introduction to speech impediments commonly found among Norwegian speakers, that Lisa realised what it was. Realised what was wrong. Why she'd felt like something wasn't right with her parents. And that they weren't the only ones. Others too. Truls and Trym. And Beatrize. Actually, now that she thought about it, pretty much everyone around her was affected. And this realisation didn't just make the hair on her head stand up, but even the fine, practically invisible hairs on her forearms.

Stork Eaters, Moa Weevils and Monster Ants

"DO YOU REMEMBER yesterday when Doctor Proctor said first 'sock thief' and then 'speech impediment'?" Lisa asked during break. She and Nilly were standing on top of a snowdrift in the playground and gazing down at the other kids, who were excitedly discussing Hallvard Tenorsen and Funny Voices. "And yesterday my parents said 'teasher' instead of 'teacher.' And 'vee' instead of 'we.' Doesn't that seem like a speech impediment?"

"That could just be a coincidence," Nilly said. "Maybe they just couldn't quite make the sounds right for whatever reason. Like they were having an off day or something, you know."

"But think about it," Lisa said. "Haven't you noticed that in the last few days, almost everyone has started saying 'sh' when they should be saying 'ch'?"

Nilly thought about it.

"Now that you mention it," he said, "actually, my mum did ask me to pick up some 'sheddar sheese' at the store. And my sister called me a 'chrimp' instead of a shrimp."

"But that's the other way around."

"My sister isn't normal."

"And one other thing," Lisa said. "Do you know what they said on the news last night?"

"That in a global poll, women had selected Nilly as man of the year?" Nilly suggested helpfully.

"No. That people have been losing more socks than usual."

"Oh no," Nilly said. "Sock thieves. You think . . . ?"

"I think something's happening, Nilly. And I think Doctor Proctor knows something he's not telling us."

"Quit scaring me, Lisa."

"I can feel it, Nilly! That thing with the missing *O* on the school banner, the wet sock footprints. What are we going to do?"

"We're going to have to tell an adult."

"But the adults are the ones talking about 'sheddar sheese' and traveller's 'shecks' and 'sharitable' contributions. Can we really trust them?"

Nilly scratched his burnsides. Sorry, his sideburns.

"Doctor Proctor," Nilly said. "He still says 'cheese' the normal way."

"And whenever we ask him what's going on, he talks his way out of it," Lisa sighed. "Nilly, we're going to have to figure this out by ourselves. Let's start at the beginning, with the invisible thing that tracked wet footprints into school."

"Hm," Nilly said. "Maybe it's time we did a little research. And of course the place to start whenever creatures are involved is A.Y.W.D.E., *Animals You Wish Didn't Exist.*"

Lisa nodded. A.Y.W.D.E. *Animals You Wish Didn't Exist.* That was the title of a six-hundred-page book that Nilly claimed was largely written by his grandfather.

AFTER SCHOOL, NILLY and Lisa raced back to Cannon Avenue.

"I have the book up in my room," Nilly said, turning around when he sensed that Lisa had stopped following him and was just standing out there on the front steps.

She had just realised that she had never been inside Nilly's house, even though they lived right across the street from each other.

"Come on," Nilly whispered.

She hesitantly stepped in the front door. She assumed Nilly was whispering because he wasn't actually allowed to have people over, and although she'd never asked him, that fit with the sense she'd always had. She supposed that was probably why she'd never bothered to ask. She had never wanted to come over here either. Nilly's mother and sister were creepier than your average family. Lisa looked around and inhaled the scents. All homes smelled like something. Well, aside from her own, of course. But that must be the same for everyone, she thought. You just can't perceive the scent of your own home. And Nilly's house smelled like . . . well, what *did* it smell like actually? Cigarettes and perfume, maybe? It certainly didn't smell the way Nilly smelled. He didn't smell like anything, just a little like Nilly.

She took off her boots and followed Nilly on her tiptoes. She saw the living room – a TV and a sofa with a big picture of his sister and mother hanging over it. Then she darted upstairs after Nilly. She ducked into his room. The walls were light blue, covered with pictures of every superhero she'd ever heard of, plus a few she hadn't heard of. A model of a glider was hanging from the ceiling on a string. Nilly was already lying on his bed, flipping through a book with a worn brown leather binding. It was almost as big as he was.

Lisa flopped down next to him.

"Let's see," Nilly said. "Sock thief."

He browsed past the animals that started with *M* and *N* and *O*, and Lisa watched him flip past descriptions and drawings of animals she definitely wished didn't exist. True, she wasn't that sure they all did exist either. If Nilly's grandfather really did write this book, it was possible that he was a little like his grandson in that he didn't take the truth too seriously if it wasn't funny enough.

They'd made it quite a way through the *S* entries. To "stork eater," an animal that looked like a brick building with a mouth like a chimney, which was clearly meant to lure storks.

"Nothing about sock thieves in here," Nilly said. "Let's look up 'speech impediments.'"

But there wasn't anything listed under "speech impediments" either.

"Hm," Nilly mused. "That's a little disappointing." Then he lit up. "On the other hand, if that creature isn't an animal you wish didn't exist, it can't be that dangerous, can it?" He moved to close the book.

"Wait!" Lisa said. "Doctor Proctor said one more thing. He didn't say the whole word, but it started with 'moon.'" She concentrated so hard her hair curled. "Moonka something! He said 'moonka.'"

Nilly flipped to the *M* entries.

"There's an entry for 'moa weevils,'" he said. "And 'monster ants.' But nothing about moonka."

"Right there!" Lisa said, pointing to the entry after "monster ants."

Nilly spelled his way through the creature's long name: "M-O-O-N C-H-A-M-E-L-E-O-N."

Lisa read aloud, as she felt her curly hair straighten itself right out, "*Chamaeleonus lunaris*. Habitat: The moon (and hopefully only there). Eats: Anything with meat on its body, preferably humans. And preferably in waffle form. Drinks: Blood and freshly steeped tea. Appearance: Unfortunately, there are no known descriptions, pictures or sketches of this gruesome creature, because anyone who has seen a moon chameleon, well, it was probably the last thing they ever saw. But it is said that you can recognise the sound of a moon chameleon approaching. It is supposed to sound like a soft, dragging sound, like socks on a wood floor and—"

"Shh!" Nilly interrupted.

They listened. And heard it. Something outside the door was approaching. A soft, dragging sound of . . .

"Get under the bed, quick!" Nilly whispered.

Lisa moved as fast as she could and as she darted underneath, she heard the door being flung open. And a voice barked, "I'm hungry!"

Lisa held her breath. Then she heard Nilly's voice: "I'm just going to finish my homework first and then I'll get started on dinner."

And then a scoffing sound: "Homework? You know

what happens to people who do too much homework? People just give them more homework!"

"I'll be there soon, Mum. Just go back to bed, okay?"

"And no fork holes in the potatoes today, or you won't get to have a birthday party."

"I never get to have a birthday party, Mum."

"Whatever."

The door closed again.

Lisa waited and waited until she was sure the mum-monster wasn't coming back. Then she crawled out. Nilly was lying on the bed, still with his turned-up nose buried in the book.

"Well?" she asked.

"It doesn't look good," Nilly said, without looking up from the book. He looked serious, more serious than Lisa had ever seen him look, more serious than a cemetery – no, than *two* cemeteries.

"Yeah, I heard," Lisa said. "No birthday party."

"I'm not talking about a *party*," Nilly said, pointing

at the book. "What's at stake here is whether any of us will ever have another birthday. Or Christmas, for that matter."

"Not . . . not Christmas," Lisa repeated, hearing the tiny little tremor in her voice. Because even though Nilly joked around about a lot of things, he would never joke about Christmas. No matter what.

"Wh-what do you mean?"

"I mean that we're looking at the end of the world," Nilly said.

The End of the World

LISA AND NILLY found Doctor Proctor in his workshop down in the cellar below the blue house. He was hammering on the soles of his balancing shoes. He lit up when he noticed them standing there.

"Come!" he said, pulling his swim goggles up onto his forehead and leading them into the laundry room.

He carefully placed the shoes on a clothesline that stretched across the length of the room, first one shoe, then the other. And sure enough, the shoes balanced there on top of the clothesline.

"Awesome!" Nilly exclaimed, so happy and excited that Lisa had to loudly clear her throat twice before he remembered why they were there and his face took on a more serious look, more appropriate given the seriousness of the situation.

"We read about the moon chameleon," Lisa said.

Doctor Proctor looked at her in terror: "You read about the . . . the . . ."

"And we understand why you didn't want to tell us about it," Lisa said. "It's not suitable for children."

"Where in the world did you read about the moon chameleon?"

"In *Animals You Wish Didn't Exist*," Nilly said. "Page three hundred and fifteen."

Doctor Proctor sank into a chair. "But the moon

chameleon is just a rumour. A ghost story from 1969, when the first moon rocket returned to Earth. The rumour went that something had come back with it. Or someone. Someone invisible. Or rather, someone that could camouflage itself to look like absolutely anything. Which is how it got the name 'moon chameleon.' People said it did the most awful things, but I forgot all that stuff until you told me about the invisible creature, the sock footprints and that spelling mistake. Everything fit, true, but I didn't want to scare you. It was just a ghost story, and as we all know, there's no such thing as ghosts." He looked up at Lisa and Nilly. "Right?"

They didn't respond.

Doctor Proctor wrung his hands. "Oh my, oh my. What did it say about it in the book?"

Nilly summarised the entry, and Lisa helped out with the parts he forgot.

"In addition to being able to blend in with any

background, it steals," Nilly said. "Simple and deliberate sock thievery. It walks right into people's homes, sneaks right past them while they're watching TV, camouflaging itself to look like a weather map or a football game and saunters right into their laundry room, where it grabs the socks out of the washing machine and puts them on. That's what we saw in the school gym – wet sock footprints."

Doctor Proctor rubbed his chin: "I've heard about the sock-stealing thing, but I never quite believed it."

Nilly sighed and pointed at Doctor Proctor's feet. "Look for yourself. You're wearing one red and one blue sock. How do you explain that?"

"Explain, schmexplain," Doctor Proctor mumbled. "I'm missing a red sock."

"Exactly. Because mysteriously one red sock vanished right out of your washing machine, right?"

"No, it burned up when I tried to dry it in the toaster."

Lisa laughed and Nilly groaned.

"Well anyway," Nilly continued. "Every day, all over the world, socks are disappearing. These daily sock mysteries remain unsolved. People look at each other in astonishment and say, 'Where in the world did they all . . .' But since they're just socks, people forget about their disappearance and don't think about it anymore. Millions of socks! A myriad of foot garments! Galaxies of sewn, knitted, crocheted, knitocheted socks!"

"But what would a . . . uh, moon creature need socks for?" Doctor Proctor asked.

"What do you think?" Nilly asked.

"Uh . . ."

"His tootsies are cold," Nilly said.

"But then wouldn't shoes be better?"

Nilly made a face. "His toes aren't made for shoes. The footprints show that moon chameleons have the longest, sharpest and most unkempt toenails you can imagine. The kind that wear holes in socks right away. That's why they have to steal new ones all the time. And, what's worse, they're invincible, they don't have any vulnerabilities. Well, aside from a little bit of spelling trouble, that is."

"What did you just say?" Doctor Proctor exclaimed.

Lisa cleared her throat: "According to *Animals You Wish Didn't Exist*, moon chameleons are notoriously bad spellers."

"Really awful spellers, actually," Nilly said.

"And especially bad with double letters," Lisa said. "That's one of the few dead giveaways for a moon chameleon. When they try to camouflage themselves as a sign, let's say one that says 'Special on Vanilla Pudding,' it usually ends up reading 'Special on *Vanila Puding.*'

"V-A-N-I-L-A," Nilly spelled. "Did you catch that?"

Doctor Proctor nodded.

"And P-U-D-I . . . ," Nilly began.

"I think he's got it now," Lisa said.

"Good," Nilly said. "So, when Lisa looked at what

she thought was our marching-band banner and noticed that it said 'Dølgen Schol Marching Band,' she actually wasn't looking at the banner at all." Nilly lowered his voice. "She was looking right at a moon chameleon who was standing in front of the banner, quiet as a mouse!"

"Eeew," Doctor Proctor said.

"Double eeew," Lisa said.

"But what about speech impediments?" Doctor Proctor asked.

"Hypnosis," Lisa said.

"Hypnosis?"

Doctor Proctor looked first at Lisa and then at Nilly, who nodded slowly. "It's in A.Y.W.D.E.," he said. "If a camouflaged moon chameleon can look into your eyes for more than two minutes, it can hypnotise you and make you do whatever it says. The only way you can tell if someone has been hypnotised is that they'll have some type of speech impediment."

"And the only way you can make them snap out of

it," Lisa continued, "is to use something that's stronger than the hypnosis."

"Like what?"

"Like something that's even more hypnotic."

"Or you can scare the bejeezus out of them," Nilly said, baring his teeth at them. "Grrr!"

"Hm," Doctor Proctor said. "I can see that you read the entry very carefully."

Nilly and Lisa nodded.

"And that you've also understood that the speech impediments, misspellings and sock thefts are not why this creature ended up in this book."

They shook their heads. Lisa closed her eyes and concentrated.

"Page three hundred and sixteen," she said, and started quoting: "No one knows where the moon chameleon lives here on Earth, but we do know they avoid daylight. If you should be so unfortunate as to see a moon chameleon in broad daylight, it means that something awful is going to happen. Something super-awful, actually. Something ultra-massively super-awful, to be completely precise. Or to be completely, totally, absolutely ultra-precise: the end of the world."

It was so quiet in the cellar for a few seconds that you could have heard a pin fall into a haystack of dry grass. If not something even quieter. Then Doctor Proctor nodded gloomily. "The end of the world. That's what the rumours used to say back then, too."

"Yeah, well," Nilly said. "Let's look at the bright side of all this. If the end of the world weren't upon us, we wouldn't have this opportunity to save the world now, would we?"

"Ugh," Doctor Proctor said with a shudder. Then he glanced out the cellar window and noticed that it was already dark. "This was such unpleasant business, I think we ought to head up to the kitchen and have ourselves some jelly!"

* * *

AT THAT MOMENT one of the two sentries on duty at the gatehouse in front of the Royal Palace, which is a large, yellow, stuccoed-brick building in the middle of Oslo, pricked up his ears and stared at the open snow-covered square in front of him.

"Hey, Gunnar, did you hear something?" he asked, running his finger over his handlebar mustache.

"What did you hear, Rolf?" his colleague asked, tugging on his Fu Manchu mustache.

"It sounded like someone just walked by in front of us."

"I don't see anyone," Mr Fu Manchu said, staring out into the darkness. Then he turned towards the facade of the building, where there were lights on in only one lone window. "Well, at any rate, it wasn't the king. He's still up, working on his crossword puzzles."

"Look!" Mr Handlebar said.

Fu Manchu turned around. His colleague pointed at something in the snow in front of them. Fu Manchu pulled off his black uniform hat with that stupid tassel

on top that looked like a horse's tail, and bent down. "Looks like dog footprints," he said.

"A dog that hasn't had its toenails clipped in a long time," Handlebar said.

"And walks on only two legs," Fu Manchu said.

"Yup," Handlebar said with a yawn. "People do such weird things with their dogs these days."

"Excuse me," a man said in a thick Swedish accent.

The two guards looked up.

In front of them stood a tall man with blond hair, dressed in something that looked sort of like an admiral's uniform. A large van with the words MAJOR MOVERS painted on the side was parked behind him.

"Yes?"

"I won the contest," the man said in Swedish.

"Uh, yes?"

"I'm the new president. Could you please tell the king he needs to pack? And then perhaps you could help me carry in my things?"

Hypnosis and Greater Norway

IT WAS late, but the jelly in Doctor Proctor's kitchen was only half eaten. When you got right down to it, it just wasn't a perfect night for jelly eating. Because jelly doesn't taste quite so jelly right after someone has asked the question "How do we save the world from doom?"

It was quiet around the table. Doctor Proctor, Lisa and Nilly had rubbed their chins a fair amount and mumbled "hm," "mm," "umph," and other noises that are helpful when you're thinking, and which can also be made without opening your mouth.

Then – finally – Doctor Proctor said "exactly" twice and then "precisely," as if he were agreeing with himself. Then he straightened up in his chair and looked at Nilly and Lisa.

"The first thing we have to do is find out how people are being hypnotised; then we can stop it from happening to us."

"And how are we going to do that?" Lisa asked.

"The scientific process," Doctor Proctor said. "We draw up a list of some people we know have been hypnotised and find out what they all have in common. And then we draw up a list of people who have *not* been hypnotised and what *they* have in common. And then the thing that all the hypnotised people have in common that the nonhypnotised people have in common that they haven't got in common will be the cause of the hypnotisation. Did you follow that?"

"Of course," Nilly said.

Lisa repeated Doctor Proctor's long explanation to herself a couple of times. "I think so," she said. "But just to be sure, maybe you could explain it to me, Nilly?"

"Uh-huh," Nilly said. "Well, it's like this . . . it's just so ingenious . . . that perhaps, well, could you explain it, Doctor Proctor?"

"Sure. Let's say that everyone who says 'sheddar sheese' instead of 'cheddar cheese' drank milk in the last week. And let's say that one of the things that everyone who says 'cheddar cheese' has in common is that they didn't drink milk—"

"Then it was something in the milk that hypnotised them," Lisa said.

"Exactly," said Doctor Proctor. "The scientific process."

"The spitting image of the scientific process," Nilly said, pushing a small helping of jelly over to Perry, who seemed totally uninterested in it.

"If we assume that most people now have a speech impediment, we can make a list of who doesn't have one," the professor said.

"Us three," Lisa said. "And Mrs Strobe."

"And Galvanius," Nilly said.

"That's plenty," Doctor Proctor said. "So then what do the five of us have in common aside from the fact that we don't have a speech impediment?"

They thought for a long time.

"We don't smoke, drink or tell lies," Nilly said.

The other two raised their eyebrows at him.

"Uh, we don't smoke or drink, that is," Nilly corrected.

"Not so fast," Doctor Proctor said. "I enjoy the occasional cigar, actually. And every once in a while a glass of red wine."

"Jelly!" Nilly yelled. "I'm absolutely positive that Mrs Strobe said one time that she likes jelly."

"But we don't know if Galvanius likes it," Lisa said. "That's the problem. We don't know anything about him. Just that he's rather odd."

"Wait a minute," Nilly said. "Doctor, when we told you that Galvanius had fallen asleep in class, you said something about him being a creature. Does that mean you know him?"

"He and I studied in Paris together at the same time," Doctor Proctor said. "I was studying chemistry and he was studying biology, but we don't need to get into that now."

"Come on!" Nilly said eagerly. "What's the deal with Mr Hiccup?"

"It's just that this one day he was so foolish as to help himself to the things that were on my shelf in the refrigerator we all shared. Need I say more?"

"Yes!" Lisa and Nilly cried in unison.

Doctor Proctor sighed. "Gregory drank from a jug of what he thought was orange juice, but was actually a strength tonic I was working on."

"A strength tonic!" Nilly exclaimed. "Cool! What was in it?"

"Nothing much. Just a mixture of different bodily fluids." Doctor Proctor squeezed one eye shut and started counting on his fingers. "Let's see . . . from the tiger shark mouse, the type A Norwegian lemming, and . . . yes, the endangered rhinoceros frog. I added anabolic asteroids. And finally a little super-strong Mexican thunder chili."

"To make people super-strong?"

"No, for the taste. Unfortunately, AFSSAPS, the French Health Products Safety Agency, banned the strength tonic."

"Why in the world would they do that?" Nilly

exclaimed, outraged. "It sounds great!"

"Too much FD&C E18 colouring," the professor sighed.

"But Mr Hiccup drank it anyway?" Lisa asked.

"Unfortunately," Doctor Proctor said. "And the results were . . ." He searched for the right way to put it. ". . . interesting. I'm afraid that's why he ended up being an arts and crafts teacher instead of a biology teacher. But enough about Gregory. We need to find out how all these people are being hypnotised!"

They kept brainstorming, but didn't get anywhere.

"I give up," Nilly finally said.

"Hm," Doctor Proctor said. "Let's try thinking of something that everyone else is doing that we're *not* doing."

They started thinking again. Hard. And then a little harder. But it was no use.

"That's enough thinking for today," Doctor Proctor said with a yawn. "Let's sleep on it and talk about it again tomorrow."

LISA AND NILLY stood out on Cannon Avenue and were saying goodnight to each other when something occurred to Lisa:

"Wait! Both of my parents and your mum were hypnotised. And Truls and Trym, right?"

"Yeah . . ."

"Mr Hiccup!" Lisa exclaimed. "That's what they have in common."

"What do you mean?"

"Think about it!" Lisa whispered, looking around as if she were afraid someone might overhear them out in the darkness. "They all either went to the parent-teacher meeting with Gregory Galvanius or had him for arts and crafts."

"No way!" Nilly exclaimed. "It's true! We have to find out what happened. We need to question our parents."

"Question them?" Lisa asked. "How?"

"Third-degree interrogation, of course," Nilly said, rubbing his palms together in anticipation. "You go grill your parents, I'll grill my mum. We'll talk tomorrow. Heh, heh, heh!" And with that Nilly ran over to the door of his little yellow house, where Lisa could see the flickering light from the TV screen through the living room window. Lisa looked at her own house. *Interrogate my own parents?* she thought.

Then she womaned up, walked through the gate, in the front door and marched into the living room, where her parents were sitting in front of the TV.

"There are a couple of things I would like answers to," Lisa announced.

But her parents didn't respond or even turn to look at her. They just kept staring at the TV screen, where Lisa saw a familiar face.

"You guys have been hypnotised," Lisa said loudly and clearly.

"Shh," her commandant father said.

"Shh," her commandant mother said.

"Did Mr Hic – I mean Mr Galvanius do this?" Lisa asked.

"Quiet, Lisa," her mother said. "Can't you see? Our president is addressing the nation."

Lisa looked at the TV screen again. Then she said, "First of all, Norway is a parliamentary democracy. We don't have a president. We have a king and a prime minister. And second of all, that guy isn't the president of anything. That's just Hallvard Tenorsen."

Her parents turned around to look at her, their faces pale and serious. In unison they gasped, *"Just?!"*

"Yes," Lisa said. "He's a . . . uh . . . a singing chiropractor from Jönköping, Sweden."

"Lisa," her mother said in that tone that told Lisa she was about to be chewed out. "I asked you to pay more attention to the news. President Hallvard Tenorsen was elected president of Norway and all its territories . . ." Her mother glanced at the clock. ". . . four hours ago. Where have you been? On the moon?"

"In a way," Lisa mumbled. "How did this happen?"

"They asked the viewing audience to call in and vote," her father said. "Tenorsen won and has already moved into the Royal Palace in Oslo. The prime minister, the whole government and the king were voted out and have to go home. Now President Tenorsen gets to make the decisions."

"The singing Swedish chiropractor is making decisions on behalf of our whole country?" Lisa asked in disbelief.

"Hallelujah," her mother said.

"But what about the king? He *lives* in the Royal Palace. That's his home."

"He's gone into exile abroad," her father said.

"Where did he go?" Lisa asked.

"R.S.T."

"Arresty?" Lisa repeated, trying to remember where that was from geography class.

"The Republic of South Trøndelag," her father replied. "He has a summer cabin up there."

"Um," Lisa replied, "but South Trøndelag is a county in Norway."

"Obviously not," her father replied.

"Um, hello?" Lisa continued. "South Trøndelag? Known for great salmon fishing? South Trøndelag is a part of Norway, Dad."

Her father just said, "Shh!"

"I need to know if Gregory Galvanius hypnotised you guys!" Lisa protested.

But her parents were once again engrossed in Tenorsen's speech.

"Norway is an itty-bitty, little country," Tenorsen said in all seriousness. "And yet — as a poet once said — it is the land of heroes. Which means that our country can sometimes feel a little, well, small. But I promise that I — with your help — will make it *bigger*. Greater Norway will soon be as big as all the other great empires of the world."

"Greater Norway?" Lisa asked. "He changed the name of our country?"

"Shh!" Her parents hushed her in unison.

Tenorsen raised his voice: "Greater Norway and its territories and colonies will soon extend from a desert in the south to a pole in the north. At least!"

Lisa heard cheering and applause coming from the TV, but she thought that was weird because she couldn't see an audience, just Tenorsen sitting at a little desk that looked suspiciously like the one the news anchor usually used.

"Now, perhaps it sounds like I'm planning on making all the decisions unilaterally," Tenorsen said.

"But clearly that isn't the case. After all, we're living in a dictatorship – sorry, ha ha, obviously I mean a democracy! *Everyone* gets to decide. All I'll do is issue a *presidential recommendation*, which should by no means be confused with a command. My first presidential recommendation is that everyone should do as I say. And it goes without saying that if you don't support the idea, just let me know."

Tenorsen smiled broadly into the camera.

"Yes, I very simply want to *encourage* everyone who doesn't agree with me to let me know. Anyone who feels like the president shouldn't make decisions at all can call the number shown on the screen now. Call and leave your name and address so I can . . . can . . ."

Tenorsen's facial expression had changed. He wasn't smiling anymore. His blond hair had slipped down over his forehead, and his eyes gleamed as if he had a pair of headlights in his head instead. But then his face relaxed and he smiled that I-won-the-presidential-election smile again: ". . . discuss the matter with you."

Applause from the invisible audience.

"That doesn't sound good," Lisa said.

"Nonsense," her commandant father said.

"Hogwash," her commandant mother said.

"And while you contemplate the issue," Tenorsen said, "we'll sing a song. Because singing fosters community and solves all problems. Think about that. We'll sing the traditional patriotic Norwegian song 'Among Hills and Mountains.'"

"I'm going to go to bed," Lisa said. "Our class is having a ski day tomorrow."

Her mother turned and looked at her in astonishment. "Aren't you going to sing along?"

Lisa shook her head. "I prefer marching bands."

When Lisa was in bed, watching Nilly's shadow theatre in the bedroom window across the street, she could hear "Among Hills and Mountains" echoing up from the living room. And when she closed her eyes, she could hear it emanating from all the houses on Cannon Avenue. She could picture the light from the TV screens flickering on people's faces as they reverently followed their beloved president's directions. Not just on Cannon Avenue, and not just in Oslo. But throughout all of Greater Norway. And its affiliated territories and colonies.

Hill Record and Reverse

"MY MUM AND sister laughed themselves silly when I asked if they felt hypnotised," Nilly said, once he and Lisa had tramped up to the top of the ski slope on their skis. They stood in line with the other kids and waited for their turn. Everyone was wearing a bib with a start number on it. Lisa had number twelve, and Nilly had asked for number thirteen.

"My mum and dad didn't even respond," Lisa said dejectedly. "They just wanted to watch TV."

"Number eight!" Mrs Strobe yelled from the bottom of the ski jump that she and Gregory Galvanius had built on the middle of the hillside.

Number eight was Trym. He peered down the hill.

"You do it," he said to Truls, who was number nine. "I don't feel like it today."

"Me either," Truls said with a yawn.

Then they pushed number ten, Ulrik, into place. Ulrik was still holding a slice of toast in his hand and his mouth was full, but he was so paralysed with fear that he just stood there, his skis locked into the tracks leading to the jump, slowly gathering speed. Finally he realised he was going to have to do something, so he tossed his toast aside and flung himself to the side. But a little too late. He sailed off the edge of the jump ramp in a sort of tipped-over-sideways position and landed in a sort of sideways spread-eagle position, making an Ulrik-shaped dent in the powdery snow next to the ramp. This earned him wild cheers and laughter as Galvanius helped him rearrange his skis, poles, legs and arms.

"Thirteen feet!" Galvanius yelled. "Style points: zero point zero! Still in eighth and last place!"

More laughter.

"Number . . . let me see . . . eleven!" Mrs Strobe yelled.

Beatrize got ready.

"We're going to have to expose Galvanius on our own," Nilly said. "We have to spy on him and get proof of what he's doing."

"Spy on him how?"

"We'll follow him when he goes home today. Find out where he lives, watch what he does. You know, basic standard spy work. Child's play."

Beatrize started her jump and they followed her with their eyes. She took off from the edge of the ramp, swayed elegantly through the air and made a neat landing quite a ways down the slope.

"Thirty-three feet!" Galvanius yelled. "Style points: nineteen, nineteen and a half! She takes the lead!"

Applause from the class.

"Number twelve!" Mrs Strobe yelled.

"Your turn," Nilly said. "Here, take a little of this." He held out his hand. It contained a small bag labelled "Doctor Proctor's Fartonaut Powder."

"Fart powder!" she whispered. "Nilly, you're crazy!" She grabbed the bag and stuffed it back into his pocket before anyone else saw it.

Nilly shrugged and said, "All the more for me."

"That's cheating, Nilly!"

"Cheating?" Nilly asked, cocking his head to the side. "And what do you call Beatrize bringing special jumping skis that her father had a professional ski waxer prepare and wax for her? While I have to compete on these?"

He nodded down at his own blue plastic mini-skis and held up his grandfather's old wooden ski poles that he'd had to saw off to make short enough. And Lisa had to agree that with equipment like that it was no surprise that Nilly was in last place, by quite a bit, after the cross-country portion of the competition. Hopelessly far behind Beatrize.

"We don't have all day, number twelve!" shouted Mrs Strobe.

Lisa pushed off. She took off softly, jumped, swayed as her skis wobbled a little, but made a clean, steady landing and turned off onto the flat area at the bottom of the jumping slope.

"Twenty-eight feet!" Galvanius yelled excitedly. "Style points: eighteen and a half, nineteen. Still in third place!"

"Number thirteen!"

Lisa turned to look back up at the top of the slope, where she saw an elf-like silhouette who was already up to speed. A hush had fallen over the class, as if everyone knew that something unusual was about to happen. They knew this quite simply because Nilly was Nilly and you could always be rather sure that something unusual would happen if he were involved. And Lisa knew that this would be a little more unusual than usual because in the hush she heard Nilly counting down "Four, three, two, one . . ." which is how long it takes from when you swallow a bag of Doctor Proctor's Fartonaut Powder until you cut the cheese with the strength and noise of a flock of three hundred thousand wildebeests and eighteen water buffaloes all farting in unison.

"Zero!"

Nilly had reached the edge of the jump ramp. Lisa covered her ears.

The explosion was deafening and was followed by a

brief, but violent, snowstorm. Afterwards everyone brushed the snow away from their eyes and blinked in confusion, looking around at the ski slope and at the thick spruce forest that surrounded them on all sides. But both the little red-haired boy and the ski jump that Mrs Strobe and Mr Galvanius had built were gone. Obliterated. Levelled to the ground.

"Nilly!" Mrs Strobe yelled, slowly rotating like a, well, like a very slowly rotating strobe light.

"Nilly!" Gregory Galvanius yelled.

"Where are you?" Mrs Strobe yelled. She was so desperate that her glasses had slid all the way down to the tip of her nose.

"Here!" yelled a voice from somewhere in the woods. Everyone turned and watched the itty-bitty, red-haired boy pushing his way out from between the enormous snow-covered trees with his poles. His smile was so big it looked like it might split his head in two.

"Wh-what were you doing in the woods?" asked a bewildered but also clearly relieved Mrs Strobe.

"Landing after my jump," Nilly said. He took off his orange hat, checked that Perry was still where he was supposed to be, brushed the snow off his hat and carefully put it back on. "I almost nailed the Telemark landing. My feet were a little too close together, but my posture was great."

Everyone stared mutely at Nilly, who was poling his way over to Beatrize.

"Here you go – a consolation prize for coming second. I plucked it off the top of the tallest spruce in there."

Beatrize stared with her mouth hanging open at the pinecone he handed her.

THE REST OF the jumping competition was cancelled since they didn't have a ramp anymore and, since they were so far north and it was winter, the sun was already sinking behind the trees. Gregory Galvanius stayed behind to clean up while the kids followed along behind Mrs Strobe in the groomed cross-country ski tracks, like ducklings following their mother. Nilly made sure he and Lisa were at the end.

"We have to sneak away," he whispered.

"Why?" Lisa asked.

"If we're going to spy on Mr Galvanius today, we have to start now so we don't lose him."

Lisa nodded. They lagged behind and when everyone else rounded a bend and disappeared from sight behind a grove of trees, Lisa and Nilly turned around and skied as quickly as they could back along the same trail they'd just come on.

As they approached the open clearing where the ski slope was, they heard someone mumbling.

"It's Galvanius," Lisa whispered.

They hid behind some spruce trees and peeked out. Mr Hiccup was sitting on a sled, bending forwards over the radio he had used to play music for the class. Beside him was a stack of folded ski bibs with numbers on them and the START and FINISH banners. He was cradling his head in his hands, and it sounded like he was repeating the same three words over and over again.

"What is he saying?" Nilly whispered.

"Shut up!" Lisa urged. "Then maybe we could hear him."

"And if you weren't so busy telling me to shut up, maybe we could hear then."

"Shh!"

"Double shh!"

"Triple shh!"

"As many *shh*s as you can say plus one!"

Lisa gave up. And listened.

"Do you hear that?" Nilly whispered.

"Yeah," Lisa said. "He's saying 'I . . . am . . . invisible.'"

"That's our proof! The man is a moon chameleon!"

That very instant Mr Galvanius raised his head, and Lisa and Nilly jumped back to hide behind the tree trunk.

"Did he hear us?" Nilly whispered.

"Shh!" Lisa said.

"Double shh!"

"Music?" Lisa asked.

Nilly listened. "It's De Beetels."

The music was coming from the radio:

Yelp! I need a bandage.

Yelp! Not just any bandage . . .

THEY STUCK THEIR heads out from behind the trunk.

"Where's Galvanius?" Lisa asked.

They didn't see anything.

"Did you feel that?" Nilly asked.

"What?"

"That shaking," Nilly said. "Like something heavy just landed on the ground."

"Duck!" Lisa said.

It was Mr Galvanius. He was suddenly herring-boning on his skis up over the hilltop, from the direction where the jump had been before Nilly farted it to smithereens. He grasped the rope attached to the sled with the radio on it, pulling everything along behind him and disappearing into the woods towards the parking lot.

"Come on!" Lisa said, starting to push herself after him with her poles.

"Wait!" Nilly said. "There's just one thing I have to check first." He snowplowed down the hill in the same spot where Mr Galvanius had come herring-boning up.

When Nilly came back a minute later, he was out of breath and his eyes were wildly excited. "Mr Galvanius jumped!"

"What do you mean?"

"He jumped SUPER-FAR! That shaking we felt was him landing."

"What are you saying? There isn't even a jump there anymore."

"And still he jumped more than one hundred and fifty feet! I saw where his ski tracks disappeared. And they didn't start again until down at the end of the clearing. A hundred-and-fifty-foot jump without a ramp, Lisa. That's just not humanly possible!" Nilly lowered his voice. "From now on, we have to do our spying with the utmost caution. Because we're not dealing with a human being, but some sort of creepy, creepy creature."

NILLY AND LISA skied as fast as they could, but they didn't catch up to Mr Galvanius until he was in the parking lot. They waited between two cars and watched him lift the sled and the start numbers into a dusty old green station wagon, which was parked so that they had a good view of the back. Then he climbed in and started the car, which spluttered and spat out black exhaust.

"What do we do?" Lisa asked. "We're going to lose him."

"Not if I have anything to do with it," said Nilly, who did actually have something to do with it. He handed Lisa his ski poles, skated over to the car on his short plastic skis, squatted down and grabbed the car's back bumper.

The engine made some ugly choking sounds, which Lisa realised meant that Mr Galvanius was trying to put the car in reverse. Reverse!

"Watch out!" Lisa shouted. "He's going to back—!"

But it was too late. The green car backed out of the parking spot, right over Nilly, who disappeared.

"Oh no!" Lisa wailed. But when the car turned and started moving forwards, Nilly appeared again, still holding firmly onto the bumper. Mr Galvanius drove across the parking lot towards the main road with Nilly in tow. But as the car approached the school bus the teachers had rented for the class ski day, Mrs Strobe came over and flagged Mr Galvanius down by waving her hands.

Lisa saw him roll down his driver's side window and heard Mrs Strobe's voice exclaim, "Lisa and Nilly are missing! We have to look for them!"

Mr Galvanius was already getting out of his car, and Lisa realised they were about to be discovered. Something had to be done. And it might require doing something Lisa intensely disliked: lying. But since what was ultimately at stake here was the end of the world, she had no choice.

"Hey!" Lisa cried out, slipping out from between the parked cars and waving with the ski poles, both her own and Nilly's sawed-off ones.

"Lisa!" Mrs Strobe yelled. "Where have you been?"

"We took a shortcut," Lisa said, using her poles to

pull herself closer so that they wouldn't come towards her, which would bring them past the back of the car and result in their discovering Nilly. "We got here way ahead of you. Nilly got tired of waiting so he, uh, took a cab back."

"A cab?"

"Yeah, he had to get back for a . . . uh, an important meeting."

"What kind of meeting?" Mrs Strobe asked slowly.

"With a . . . uh, chorus," Lisa said. She could hear how her voice revealed how little practise she had at lying.

"A chorus?" Mrs Strobe's eyebrows pressed themselves together into a scary V just over the bridge of her nose.

"Yeah, a chorus from America," Lisa said, swallowing. "They want him to be their conductor."

Out of the corner of her eye, she saw Nilly crouching behind the car. And on the other side, she saw the

bus with Beatrize and her friends, who were all press-
ing their incredulous faces against the windows.

"I'm going to have to have a talk with Nilly about
this tomorrow," Mrs Strobe said. "Come on, we're
going."

"Okay," Lisa said, following Mrs Strobe onto the
bus. Lisa found an empty seat and gazed out of the
window. Mr Galvanius got back in his car and revved
his engine.

"Hey, Lisa?"

Lisa looked up. It was Beatrize, who asked, "Hey,
uh, could I, uh, sit next to you?"

Lisa shrugged in response and looked out of the
window again.

"So, uh," said Beatrize, who pressed herself into the
seat. "Since you know Nilly, and he's going to, like,
conduct this American chorus . . ."

"Mm."

"Do you think it would be okay if vee kind of just

went along . . . you know?"

"Why?"

"Well . . . then vee could be on American TV and vee'd be celebrities!"

"I see," Lisa said, watching Mr Galvanius drive away. And there – in the cloud of black exhaust behind his car – she thought she could just make out someone's red hair.

Basic, Standard
Spy Work

LISA WENT TO bed for the night, but couldn't fall asleep. There was no light in Nilly's bedroom window. What had happened? She wondered for a while if she shouldn't say something to her parents, but of course they were hypnotised. She had decided to sneak over to Doctor Proctor's and ask him what they should do, but a sudden bang made Lisa jump, rising three inches off her mattress. She stared at the dark windowpane, which was still rattling from the impact. What was left of a snowball slid down the glass. Truls and Trym? No, they were much too cowardly to throw snowballs at a house where the Commandant lived. She leaped up in bed and stared out. And there, in the light of a lone streetlight, stood a guy with a coal black face, staring up at her. Her heart jumped more than three inches from pure joy. It was Nilly! Lisa turned on her light so he could see her.

Nilly waved and motioned for her to come down. Lisa threw on her clothes and snuck down the stairs. As she tiptoed past the living room she heard a familiar TV voice say: "Norway is too small, my dear citizens. In my capacity as the president of Greater Norway, I called the king of Denmark and asked him if it would be okay for us to take over his country. Unfortunately, he was not in favour of this. And as if

that weren't enough, he got all mean and called us mountain monkeys and said we 'ought to just stay up here in our trees. If you can even grow trees that far north, that is.'"

Lisa pulled on her boots in the hall and put on her jacket.

"The first question," Hallvard Tenorsen thundered from the living room, "is whether we – the proud people of Norway – are going to just let him get away with such a cheeky comment. The second question is whether the king of Denmark means to imply, since we're apparently monkeys, that he can just waltz over here and populate Norway with his Danish people whose language is so garbled they all sound like they're trying to talk with potatoes in their mouths. My presidential recommendation is that we should consider striking Denmark first, before they strike us! Call in now and vote! And if you're opposed, remember to leave your name and address.

Now let's sing the national anthem. Everyone ready? And a one, and a two, and a one, two, three . . ."

Lisa grabbed Nilly's ski poles and slipped out of the house.

"I found out where he lives," Nilly said as she stepped through her front gate.

"I'm so happy to see you!" she whispered. "If your face weren't so dirty, I'd give you a hug."

"Dirty?" Nilly asked.

"Yeah, it's totally black," Lisa said, dragging her finger over his cheek to reveal a blinding milky-white stripe of freckled skin. She showed him her black fingertip.

"Must be from the exhaust," Nilly said. "Mr Galvanius needs to flush his spark plug constipators with blue oil. Beyond a doubt. Anyway, he drove straight home and parked on the street. I snuck after him and saw him go into a little brick house. So I snuck into the yard, climbed a tree outside his living room window and spied. And spied. And spied."

"What did you see?" Lisa asked, recognising that wonderful tingly feeling of excitement that always came right before adventures became truly adventurous.

"Him sleeping," Nilly said, accepting his ski poles, which Lisa was handing him.

"What?"

"Him sleeping. He filled his bathtub, undressed, climbed into the tub and slept. And slept and slept."

"He was lying in his bathtub? He's still lying in his bathtub now?"

"I've never seen so much bathing and sleeping," Nilly said. "This must certainly have been the most boring spy assignment in history. And the coldest."

"I see," Lisa said, a little disappointed that it hadn't turned out to be very adventurous after all. "And now?"

"Shift change. Perry is watching now, but it will be your turn to do the spying next."

"Spy on a man taking a bath, while he's asleep?"

"Come on," Nilly said. "It's not far, just climb onto the back of my skis."

And Lisa thought that maybe, maybe, the adventure might end up being a little adventurous if she just helped a little. So she positioned her winter boots behind Nilly's on his puny skis, braced herself by holding his shoulders and said, "Ready!"

And with that, Nilly pushed off so the ice underneath them rumbled.

THEY ARRIVED ON a street of quiet homes. The moon was shining on the little brick house Nilly stopped in front of. There were no cars or people to be seen or heard anywhere.

"Is this it?" Lisa asked.

"Yes," Nilly said, cautiously poling his way up to the front gate and putting one finger on the gatepost.

"Come on in and warm up, buddy," Nilly said.

In the moonlight, Lisa could see Perry dart up

Nilly's hand and arm and then in under his hat.

Nilly was about to open the gate when his hand suddenly stopped.

"He went out again," Nilly said.

"How do you——?" Lisa started to ask.

"Perry made this before I left," Nilly said, pointing to the freshly made spiderweb stretched between the gatepost and the gate itself. It had been pulled off and was dangling loose.

"Someone left recently," Lisa confirmed. "But where'd they go?"

In answer to her question, they heard an engine turn over a couple of times before it finally started hacking and spluttering in a familiar way.

"Quick!" Nilly said. "Back onto the skis!"

As they glided across the street, they saw that the green station wagon had already pulled out and was spewing out exhaust as it disappeared, heading towards the first intersection.

"I have longer arms," Lisa said, snatching the ski poles from Nilly. She pushed them along with the poles as hard as she could, and they started to speed up. But Mr Galvanius's car was already through the first intersection and pulling away.

"Faster!" Nilly screamed. "We're losing him!"

"This is as fast as it goes!" Lisa gasped, pumping the poles into the snow-covered street. "We have to give up!"

"No, no!" Nilly cried. "There's a stoplight coming. We can still catch him if it's red!"

"He has too much of a lead, Nilly."

"Oh yeah?" Nilly said, and pulled something out of his jacket pocket. "Here! Take the rest!"

Lisa saw that it was the bag of Doctor Proctor's Fartonaut Powder.

"No way!" she said. "Girls don't fart!"

"Yes they do, and I've seen you rip a big one before. You have to do this. The end of the world, yadda, yadda, yadda!"

"I said no! You take it!"

"Don't be fart shy now, Lisa! I'm standing *in front* of you. If I took it I would blast you right off the skis, as you well know."

Lisa was seething inside. She *hated* farting. But she hated being called fart shy even more.

"Give it here," she said, grabbing the bag. She tipped her head back and emptied the contents into her mouth.

"Ho ho ho!" yelled Nilly, doubling over with glee. "Seven, six . . ."

Way, way up ahead, ahead of the tiny dot of a car, Lisa thought she glimpsed a light. A green light. She could already feel her stomach tickling and boiling and bubbling.

"Five, four . . ." said Nilly.

No, wait, now the light was yellow. And the amount of pressure that had built up in her stomach made it feel more or less like she'd swallowed a blown-up balloon.

"Three, two, one."

The light ahead of them turned red. Lisa could see the brake lights on Mr Galvanius's car come on. And the balloon in her stomach wasn't just fully inflated now, it was ready to burst.

"Hold on tight!" Nilly cheered. "Lift off!"

And with that came the explosion. Lisa thought she felt the seat of her pants tear as a warm jet stream of gas hissed and blasted out. And as if they had a rocket motor behind them – which in a way they did – they zoomed forwards. The gardens, the houses and the intersections flickered past. But gradually the stream of gas abated, as did their speed.

"Hard landing!" Nilly yelled.

Then seven things happened in quick succession.

An audible thunk could be heard as they slammed into the back of the green station wagon.

The traffic light turned from red to green.

The green station wagon started driving.

Nilly grabbed the bumper, but his hands slipped out

of his mittens, which remained stuck to the bumper. (And Nilly thought his mother and Eva would really be annoyed now. Those were the mittens they'd given him for Christmas the year before last along with the admonition that if he lost them, they'd give him a noogie, a wedgie and a knuckle sandwich.)

Nilly roared a word that unfortunately can't be printed here since this is a children's book.

Lisa swung out her right arm and ski pole so that the basket near the bottom of the pole, at the last nanofraction of a second, hooked the inside of the bumper and pulled them away after the car.

Nilly roared a word that happily *can* be printed: "Yippee!"

BOTH LISA AND Nilly were hunkered down behind the car, holding on tight to the ski pole as they were hauled through the quiet nighttime city. The black smoke from the exhaust pipe made Lisa cough a little, but actually it wasn't that bad. The skis slid over snow and icy ruts, and when Lisa looked up she saw the moon drifting across a clear nighttime sky filled with stars. And Lisa thought it had actually turned out to be a nice evening. Despite all that business about the end of the world and whatnot, it was a really nice evening.

Suddenly they heard a loud scraping sound under their skis, and the car started braking.

"What's going on?" asked Lisa, who had her hands full trying to keep her balance.

"We just drove over a manhole cover," Nilly said.

The car pulled to a stop. Lisa unhooked the ski pole from the bumper.

"Come on, Nilly!" she whispered. "We have to hide!"

Nilly snatched his mittens, which were still hanging from the bumper, and skated along behind Lisa over to the edge of the pavement. They crouched down behind a parked car.

Mr Galvanius got out of the green station wagon.

"Look," Lisa whispered. "He's only wearing his dressing gown!"

"And his Vegard Ulvang commemorative Olympic cross-country skiing socks," Nilly muttered. "That just reeks of moon chameleon if you ask me."

They followed him with their eyes as he walked over to the manhole cover they'd driven over. The warm air from the sewers underneath had melted the snow and ice on top of the manhole cover. Mr Galvanius reached down into the holes in the heavy iron circle and flipped it up. A second later he was gone.

"He crawled down into the sewer!" Nilly said.

"What in the world is he going to do down there?" Lisa asked. "Maybe he felt way too clean after all that bathing?"

"Let's find out," Nilly said, undoing his skis. "Quick!"

He darted over to the manhole cover on his short legs and tried to pick it up the way Mr Galvanius had, but it was too heavy.

"Help me, would you?" he hissed between clenched teeth as he tugged and pulled.

Lisa got her fingers down into the holes and tried her best to pick it up, but the lid wouldn't budge.

"Who would've thought that Mr Hiccup was so strong?" Nilly hissed, pulling so hard his face turned completely red.

Lisa suddenly let go of the lid.

"What is it?" Nilly asked.

"We shouldn't go down there."

"Why not?" Nilly asked.

"Anaconda," Lisa said.

"Anna Conda?"

"Anaconda! The snake, the constrictor. Big. As in biiiiig! I don't want to have anything to do with big snakes."

Nilly let go of the lid and cocked his head to the side: "Lisa! Don't tell me you believe that old urban legend?"

Lisa gave Nilly an offended look. "Well, there's believing and then there's believing. You're actually the one who told it in the first place, Nilly. You said there's an eighteen-yard-long anaconda snake in Oslo's sewers that is so insatiable that it eats absolutely everything it encounters. Yup, you even said it actually ate you on one occasion, but that you miraculously got out of the predicament."

"I did?" Nilly said, scratching his sideburns. "Hm, I suppose I'm beginning to get forgetful. But, of course, if your source is someone as reliable as me, I have to believe you. Fine, we won't go down there. Because I don't want to have anything to do with anaconda stuff either."

They stood there for a while peering down at the black manhole cover with the even blacker holes that led down to an even, even blacker darkness that led down to the blackest of the black: Oslo's jumble of subterranean pipes and walkways where no one up here knew – or wanted to know – exactly what went on.

"Well, should we call it quits on the spying for tonight, then?" Lisa asked hopefully.

"Almost," Nilly said. He had that little smile that Lisa knew almost always meant trouble.

"What do you mean?" she asked, but she already suspected what the answer would be.

"Gregory Galvanius's house is empty. And as you know, seven-legged Peruvian sucking spiders are whizzes when it comes to picking locks."

"Nilly, no! We can't go breaking into people's houses."

"First of all, tiny little break-ins into people's houses are nothing to make a stink about when we're talking about saving the world from certain doom. Second of all, I thought we agreed that Mr Galvanius is not a person; he's a moon chameleon. And the one place we're most likely to find proof of that is in his house."

"Yeah, but . . ."

"Now's our chance, Lisa."

"Yeah, but it's not . . . we can't . . ." Lisa tried and tried, but no matter how she thought about it, Nilly was right. And she hated it when Nilly was both crazy and right at the same time, especially when it meant that her life was about to become more difficult.

"Oh slush and bother," she said. "Let's get this break-in over with, then."

"Yippee!" Nilly cried.

Break-Ins and
Love Letters

THERE WAS A little click and then Perry crawled
back out of the keyhole.

"Good job, Perry!" Nilly said. He turned the knob,
and the door to Gregory Galvanius's little brick house
slid open. Nilly set Perry on the wall next to the doorbell and gave the spider a serious look: *"Toca el timbre*

si ves al Señor Galvanius que viene, ¿de acuerdo?"

"Huh?" Lisa asked.

"I asked him to ring the doorbell if he sees Mr Galvanius coming."

"Oh yeah?" Lisa said. "What, like in spider language or something?"

"Don't be dumb. Spiders can't talk. But they know Spanish. That's what they speak in Peru."

Lisa was about to say something, but realised it wouldn't do any good. She hurried in after Nilly instead and shut the door behind them. They stood there in the dark hallway holding their breath and listening.

"What's that sound?" Lisa whispered.

"Your heart beating," Nilly whispered.

"No, listen."

"You're hearing things, Lisa. There's no one here besides us."

"There's a buzzing sound."

"Cut it out. It's just – wait! Do you hear that? There's a buzzing sound."

"Uh, yeah. That's what I just—"

"Come on!" Nilly interrupted, pulling her by the arm.

They continued down the hallway that led them past the living room and over to a door.

"It's coming from in there," Nilly said.

"Yup," Lisa said.

"Maybe you should open it?" Nilly suggested.

"Or maybe you should open it," Lisa replied.

"Rock-paper-scissors," Nilly said.

They counted to three and then showed their hands.

"Hah!" Lisa exclaimed triumphantly because she had chosen paper and Nilly had chosen rock.

"What are you hah-ing for?" Nilly asked. "Rock beats paper."

"What?"

"Didn't you hear about it? They changed the rules at the annual meeting this October."

"They?"

"Yeah, the International Rock-Paper-Scissors Association."

Lisa was going to protest, but suddenly felt like they should put this silliness behind them. She pulled the door open.

It was dark in there, but the buzzing noise was intense.

"Ow!" Lisa yelled, more because she was startled than because the little prick on her neck hurt. Nilly had obviously found the light switch, because just then the light came on in the room.

Lisa went bug-eyed. Literally.

"Mosquitoes," she said, rubbing her neck.

"And flies," Nilly added.

The bare, unfurnished room was buzzing with insects, large and small, apparently all of them able to fly. And now they all swarmed around the lone light bulb hanging from the ceiling.

Lisa slammed the door shut again.

"Odd," Nilly said.

They walked through the other rooms. It didn't take long: There wasn't anything other than a living room, a kitchen and a bathroom with a bathtub that was still full of water.

"Apart from the insect thing this place really isn't that weird," Nilly said after they got back to the living room.

"Nope," Lisa said. "Except for something that *isn't* here."

"Yup," Nilly said and flopped down, exhausted, onto the sofa. "The guy doesn't have a TV. That's almost a little creepy."

"I meant a *bed*. Where is Mr Galvanius's bed?"

"Hm," Nilly said, putting his hands behind his head and closing his eyes. "Maybe he sleeps on the sofa."

"But he has a bedroom, so why—" Lisa stopped

all of a sudden and then exclaimed, "He sleeps in the bathtub!"

"Yeah, that's what I said."

"I mean: He *sleeps* there. Every night!"

"Quit joking around," Nilly said with a yawn. "Think about what that would do to his back. We're talking prolapsed discs, sciatica, luxated funny bone . . ."

"You're the one who says he isn't a normal person," Lisa said. "Right?"

But Nilly didn't respond. His mouth had slid open and at regular intervals was emitting a sound like a gearshift that someone was trying to put in reverse. He was snoring.

OUTSIDE THE HOUSE it was very still.

Then the gate made an almost inaudible creaking sound.

Then more stillness.

Then a whistling sound, like a lasso being thrown through the darkness. Followed by a little smack, as if something wet had hit the side of the house.

After that the same whistling sound and then finally a bigger smack, like a pair of jaws snapping shut.

And then stillness again.

LISA TOOK A quick tour of the living room while she listened to Nilly's soft, regular snoring. There weren't any pictures on the walls, but now she'd reached the desk. And on it sat a piece of paper that someone had started writing on. She picked it up and read it.

> Dear Rosemarie,
>
> Please forgive me for approaching you in such a forward manner, but what I'm about to write is something I've been carrying with me for so long it just has to be said. I love

you, Rosemarie. There, I said it. ~~I've loved~~
~~you since the first time I saw you.~~ There
were two reasons that I never dared tell you
before. The first is that I haven't been able
to deal with the rejection that I must obviously
be the result ~~of my telling you I love you.~~ Of
course a poor slob like me could never win the
love of a woman like you, Rosemarie. That
much is obvious. But there's also another
reason. And that is that I have turned my
back on love. Because love has never given me
anything but pain. She was from Austria.
Her name was Agnes. She left me because
she thought we didn't have anything in
common. She moved back home to Salzburg,
started dating a guitarist named Bruno,
dyed her hair blonde, bought high-heeled
boots and started singing in his Austrian
dance orchestra. They became world famous

and I started drinking and moved to an out-of-the-way place where I got a job as a teacher. A bad teacher. I teach arts and crafts, which I don't actually know anything about. But I just wasn't up to teaching biology, because I can't handle cuting up dead frogs.

Lisa felt the sweat start beading up on her forehead. She stared at one word: "cuting." With just one *t* where there should have been two. That meant one of three things: That Gregory Galvanius was a bit of a sloppy speller, which happens. To err is human. That this wasn't written by a human at all, but rather by a moon chameleon! That "cutting" was spelled correctly in the actual letter, but that a moon chameleon was standing in between Lisa and the letter right now!

Lisa dropped the letter with a little scream.

Nilly emitted a small grunt over on the sofa.

And right then the light went out.

Lisa flung her hands over her own mouth to stop herself from screaming any more. She stared straight into the darkness, but didn't see anything, just heard. Heard Nilly's soft snoring plus something else. A sound that made her hair stand on end, first the hair on her arms, then on the back of her neck and then on her head. Hiccups. She heard familiar, croaking hiccups. And they weren't coming from outside; they were here. Here in the room.

"N-N-Nilly," Lisa stuttered, trying to control the trembling in her voice. But instead the trembling just spread to the rest of her body until she felt like she was vibrating like a jackhammer. Because now she could also make out something in the darkness: A pair of large, bulging eyes that glowed, and with eyelids that slid slowly up and down over them.

"Nilly!!!" Lisa howled.

The snoring stopped all of a sudden. There were a

couple of grunts, and then a sleepy "What's going on?"

The voice that responded wasn't Lisa's. But a squeaky, whispery voice that lisped, "What's going on – *hic!* – is that you're about to be eaten!"

It was Gregory Galvanius's voice.

Lisa felt something cold and slimy curl around her neck and squeeze. A hand. But not a human hand.

"Help!" Lisa screamed, flailing her arms, but the hand just tightened its grip.

"Double help!!" Nilly screamed.

"There is no help for – *hiccup!* – thieves." Mr Galvanius laughed a squeaky and very ominous laugh.

And just then the light came on.

"There is *too* help," said a familiar voice. And in the doorway stood a familiar tall, thin figure.

"Doctor Proctor!" exclaimed Lisa in relief.

"Professor!" Nilly cheered.

"Vic – *hiccup!* – tor?" Gregory Galvanius said, tightening the belt on his dressing gown.

"Quick!" Nilly yelled, bouncing off the sofa, hopping up onto Mr Galvanius's shoulders and locking his legs around Mr Galvanius's neck. "Don't let him camouflage and get away."

"Hiccup!" Mr Galvanius whirled around as he tried to grab the pest who was clamped onto the back of his head like a vise.

"Stop, Nilly," Doctor Proctor said.

"We have to save the world from the moon chameleons!" Nilly shouted, pounding Gregory Galvanius's head with his itty-bitty fist.

"Ow! *Hiccup!* Ow!"

"Stop, I said!" Doctor Proctor shouted. "Gregory is not a moon chameleon!"

Gregory Galvanius and Nilly stopped all of a sudden, both of them.

"What did you say I – *hiccup!* – wasn't?" Mr Galvanius asked.

"A moon chameleon," Doctor Proctor said.

"If he's not one of those, then what is he?" Nilly asked.

"You two detectives really haven't figured that one out yet?" the professor asked, walking over to Mr Galvanius and helping Nilly down from his shoulders.

"Maybe not," Lisa said, squinting her right eye closed. "But it's starting to become clear."

"Exactly!" Nilly said. "Or . . . uh, is it?"

"Yes," Lisa said. "He sleeps in a bathtub and actually ought to be hibernating now. He jumped one hundred and fifty feet on the ski slope with no ramp to take off from. He has a room full of insects. And there's the hiccuping, which is actually croaking. He's"—Lisa pointed her index finger at Gregory Galvanius, who looked at her in terror—"a frog!"

"A frog?!" Nilly repeated.

"A kind of frog," Doctor Proctor said, nodding in confirmation.

"A fool of a frog, caught in the act," Gregory Galvanius said, hanging his head.

"You're kidding!" Nilly laughed, looking around at everyone else. "Or . . . you're not kidding?"

In response, Gregory Galvanius opened his mouth and let his tongue roll out. And out. And out. Until it lay across the length of the room like a red carpet, well, a bluish-red carpet, all the way over to the tip of Nilly's nose. And there, at the very tip of his tongue, sat Perry, struggling to get any of his seven legs free. They were all stuck in the sticky frog-tongue mucus.

"I knew it was you when I saw this chap by my doorbell," Mr Galvanius lisped. "Take him before I eat him. He's quite a tempting morsel."

A look of disgust came over Nilly's face and he carefully plucked his spider friend off the long tongue using his thumb and index finger. Perry darted straight up Nilly's arm and neck and under his hat to safety.

Mr Galvanius rolled his tongue back up and closed his mouth with a loud *smack*.

"And now," Doctor Proctor said, clapping his hands together with a *smack* that wasn't anywhere near as loud, "I suggest we all sit down and get to the bottom of a few things. Which is to say, we have other things we need to do. And we don't have much time."

"What other things?" Mr Galvanius asked.

"The usual," Nilly said, stifling a yawn. "We have to save the world."

Waltzing King
and Frog

ONCE THEY WERE all seated around the coffee table in the living room – Doctor Proctor, Lisa, Nilly and Gregory Galvanius – Doctor Proctor explained how he had found them.

He was working on his balancing shoes and listening to the local news on the radio when Eva, Nilly's sister, called and asked if Nilly was there. Because they hadn't seen him since he left for school that morning, and his mother was waiting for him to bring her dinner in bed the way he usually did. Doctor Proctor asked her to check with Lisa and hadn't given it another thought until he heard the loud voice of Lisa's commandant father calling from the front porch of her house.

He understood, from what the angry commandant was saying, that Lisa's bed was empty, that she had disappeared. Just then the newscaster on the radio said that the residents of a home located at number 24 Andedam Road had reported hearing a violent explosion that had rattled windows throughout the neighbourhood, and had also seen a girl and something that must have been a dwarf breaking the speed limit on a pair of mini-skis. And since Doctor Proctor knew that his old college roommate from Paris lived at number 25 Andedam Road, and that Lisa and Nilly had been talking about Gregory recently, he put two and two together and came up with fartonaut powder. And decided to head down there and see what was going on.

"We have to go home and let our families know we're okay," Lisa said. "They must be worried."

"Oh, they can surely wait a little longer," Doctor Proctor said. "We have more important things to think about than worried parents."

"Yup," Nilly said. "But first we have to find out how someone turns into a frog."

"A kind of frog," Doctor Proctor said. "Why don't you explain, Gregory?"

"Alas!" Gregory alassed. "Do you want the long version or the short version?"

"The long version," Nilly and Lisa said in unison.

IT TOOK ALMOST ten minutes for Gregory to finish telling them about his childhood at the very southern tip of Norway, about his temperamental father who wanted him to be a professional volleyball player, and how he had defied his family's wishes and gone to Paris to study biology.

"That's where I met Agnes," Gregory said. "The most beautiful creature on two legs."

"Kooky?" Nilly asked. Not because he was asking if Agnes was a little nutty, but because it's hard to say "cookie" with a mouth full of cookie crumbs. Nilly held out a package of cookies, the only food in the whole house, unless you ate insects.

"No thanks," Gregory said. "Where was I?"

"In Paris."

"Right. Yeah, so I was head-over-knees in love, as they say. And then I somehow worked up the courage to invite Agnes to a concert by De Beetels. And can you believe it? She said yes! And as they were playing a song called 'She Luvs Ya,' she turned to me and said in an Austrian accent: 'It eez true, vat day are zinging, Gregory.' And then she kissed me right on the mouth, as De Beetels sang 'She luvs ya, nah, nah, nah.' That was the happiest moment of my life. The minute after that was nice, too. And the one after that. Actually, life was pretty much a long progression of wonderful moments, up until I was so careless as to drink out of that pitcher."

"A tragic misunderstanding," Doctor Proctor said.

"Misunderstanding?!" scoffed Gregory, his face turning red with rage. "Victor, you were keeping a pitcher filled with a potentially lethal beverage in our communal fridge! *Hiccup!*"

"And I'm sorry about that," Doctor Proctor said. "But you stole it from my shelf, Gregory!"

Gregory and Doctor Proctor looked at each other. Then Gregory bent his head again and admitted, "You're right. I shouldn't have done that."

"Well, at any rate, you've learned," Nilly said. "You didn't eat Perry."

"Oh, I don't eat people's pets," Gregory said. "That's over the line."

"But what happened when you drank from that pitcher?" Lisa asked.

"Yes, what did happen?" Gregory said. "I woke up that same night, covered in slime. Oozing from my own skin. I felt the Adam's apple in my throat moving up and down and felt strangely compelled to search for moths and mosquitoes and ants. The changes weren't that big in the beginning. But then I got stronger. I could jump thirty feet. Without even getting a running start. I could clean the outsides of my windows on the third floor by standing out in the yard and jumping up and down. I'd turned into a superman! I was sure Agnes would just love me even more. But then one night – oh, that fateful night . . ."

Gregory paused.

"What? What happened that night?" Lisa urged.

Gregory hid his face in his hands. "I was walking her home from the movies and was planning to kiss her. And it was going to be a good one . . ."

"Eeew," Nilly shuddered.

Gregory took a deep breath and continued. "She shrieked when I opened my mouth and rolled out my tongue. I actually hadn't really realised how long it had got. Plus it was awfully sticky. She squealed like a stuck pig. Then she ran into her House and locked her door behind her. I thought she probably needed a little time to get used to the idea of kissing a guy with a tongue that was so much longer than average. But the next day her landlord said she'd packed her bags and gone back home to Salzburg in Austria."

Gregory was quiet. He stared straight ahead and swallowed, his Adam's apple moving up and down, as if he were trying to swallow his sad reality one more time.

"Then what happened?" Lisa practically whispered.

"Then a few months passed with me hoping she would come back. Until the day I happened to turn on the TV. And there she was. With Bruno. They were singing together. And they looked so in love. Their band was called BABA, and the song was 'Waltzing King.'"

"Oh, that one is great," Lisa said, and started singing, *"You are the waltzing king . . ."*

"Stop!" Gregory howled, his hands over his ears.

"Humph." Lisa pouted, offended. "My singing isn't thaaaat bad . . ."

"Well . . ." Nilly said.

"It's not your singing. It's the *song*," said Gregory, whose face had suddenly gone ashen. "She broke my heart. I stayed in bed for three weeks after that TV show. Like a feeble, spineless dishrag, barely able to croak. And every time I started to feel better, they would play that BABA song on the radio, and I would have to lie down again. I just stayed like that until one day Victor came to my room."

Doctor Proctor shrugged. "All I did was put on a record to cheer him up."

"But it was the right *song*, Victor."

"Apparently," Doctor Proctor said. "Because he

hopped out of bed. And when I say hop, I mean he was bouncing like a rubber ball around the floor, walls and ceiling."

"It was 'She Luvs Ya' by De Beetels," Gregory said.

"I get it," Lisa said.

"You do?" Nilly asked, looking at her in surprise.

"Yeah," Lisa said. "'She Luvs Ya' reminded you of the happiest moment in your life. When Agnes kissed you. And you got your superpowers back."

Gregory nodded despondently. "And it's still like that."

"Aha!" Nilly exclaimed. "That's why you jumped one hundred and fifty feet up there on the ski slope! Because you were listening to 'She Luvs Ya.'"

"Yup. And sadly, whenever I hear BABA, I still go limp like gelatin and can't manage to do anything."

"BUT THERE'S STILL one thing I'm wondering," Nilly said. "What in the world were you doing in the sewer?"

Gregory shrugged. "Sometimes it gets a little lonely up here being a frog. Especially now, in the winter, when most of the frogs in Norway are hibernating under the ice somewhere. So sometimes I like to go hang out with the sewer frogs for a little while."

"The sewer frogs?"

"It's warm down there."

"What do you guys do?"

"Shoot the breeze. Eat a cockroach or a spider. Have a good time."

"Double eeew!" Nilly said.

"Frogs can *talk*?" Lisa asked.

"Yeah, of course," Galvanius said.

"What language do they speak, huh?"

"Froglish, of course."

"And what does it sound like?"

"Hiccup!" Gregory said. *"Hiccup, hiccup, hiccup."*

"And what does that mean?"

"'Could I have a beer, please?'"

"That's awesome!" Nilly cried, howling with laughter.

"What do frogs like to talk about?" Doctor Proctor asked.

"All kinds of stuff," Gregory said. "Tonight most of them were talking about some strange waffle-eating monkeys that have moved down into the sewers."

"Say something else in Froglish!" Nilly urged, tears of laughter still pouring from his eyes.

"Hiccup," Gregory said, and he was laughing now, too. *"Hiccup, hiccup, hiccup, hiccup, hiiiiiiiccup."*

"Which means?" Nilly asked.

"'I only speak a little Froglish, so please speak sloooooowly.'"

And with that, both Nilly and Gregory toppled over backwards on the floor in a fit of laughter. And Doctor Proctor started chuckling as well.

"What *I'm* wondering," said Lisa, who was the only

one who wasn't laughing, "is why you were sitting on the sled on the ski slope saying 'I am invisible.' That's what convinced us you were a moon chameleon."

"Oh, you heard that?" Gregory said. "I . . . uh, was talking to myself about a particular person who . . . well, I seem to be a little invisible to."

"Gregory, you're blushing!" Doctor Proctor teased. "You don't mean you've fallen in love again, do you? If you have, well, really it was about time."

"In love?" Gregory laughed an unusually giddy laugh. "No, no. *Hiccup!* I . . . uh . . . yeah, I might like someone, but – *hiccup!* – in love? Ha, ha, ha, well I never!"

The other three looked at Gregory. And if there was one thing that there was no longer any doubt about, it was that Gregory Galvanius was in love. But after reading the letter, Lisa was the only one who knew *who* he was in love with. And who Rosemarie was. But of course she didn't say anything.

"Anyway," Doctor Proctor said. "Now that we've established that Gregory isn't a moon chameleon and also hasn't been hypnotised, I think we should ask him to help us save the world."

"Yes!" Lisa and Nilly agreed.

"What's all this business about moon chameleons?" Gregory asked.

They explained all the business about moon chameleons to him. Afterwards, Gregory summarised: "So, a moon chameleon can disguise itself to look like a person, like any kind of background, basically like anything at all. They eat human flesh more or less the way we Scandinavians eat meatballs. They struggle with double letters, steal socks and hypnotise people to say stuff like 'sheep sheese' instead of 'cheap cheese.' And in this book you mention, it also says that if you see a moon chameleon in broad daylight, it means that something horrendously bad will happen."

"Unspeakably, appallingly bad," Nilly corrected.

"And you're telling me that you saw moon chameleon tracks in broad daylight, and that this means the end of the world is coming?"

Nilly and Lisa nodded.

Gregory laughed. "It all sounds ridiculous. Don't you think?"

Lisa thought about it. And realised that Gregory was right. She wasn't so convinced anymore. Actually, when you got right down to it, nothing very doomlike had occurred. No earthquakes, no volcanic eruptions, not even so much as a meteor shower.

But Doctor Proctor was the one who responded. "I think it's time you guys knew about the rest."

Everyone turned to look at him.

"The part that's not in the book," Doctor Proctor

said with a gloomy expression, "but was included in the rumours I heard in Paris."

"Is it sc-sc-scary?" Lisa whispered.

"Actually, you're supposed to be eighteen to hear this," Doctor Proctor said. "So maybe we ought to turn on a few more lights before I proceed."

Scary, Really Bad News

DOCTOR PROCTOR LOOKED somberly at the others gathered around the coffee table in Gregory's living room.

"I've put off telling you this as long as I could. After all, it's all just rumours."

"And what are the rumours?" Lisa asked.

"That the moon chameleons are coming to eat us," Doctor Proctor said.

"*Eat* us?" Lisa, Nilly and Gregory all asked in unison.

Doctor Proctor nodded, his facial expression gloomy. "The rumours in Paris went like this: Mars used to be inhabited by Martians . . ." he began.

"Sounds logical," Nilly said. "I mean, if anyone was going to live there, that's who you'd expect it to be."

"No one lives there," Doctor Proctor said. "The moon chameleons ate them all up, because that's what they do. They travel from planet to planet devouring any intelligent life they encounter. And the most intelligent life on earth is . . . well, us."

"I agree," said Nilly, who didn't seem to have noticed how frightened Lisa and Gregory were.

"By us, I mean all people," Doctor Proctor said.

"But – but—," Lisa stammered, "why haven't we ever heard of a single person being eaten, then?"

"If I'm right, it's because moon chameleons are

pretty clever beasts," Doctor Proctor said. "They're planning something, something that will keep us from realising what's going on until it's too late."

"If what you're saying is right, we need to find out what their plan is," Gregory said.

"And then those of us who haven't been hypnotised by the moon chameleons need to organise some sort of resistance movement," Doctor Proctor said.

"A resistance movement!" Lisa exclaimed. "Like what they had in World War Two!"

"Well, we're out of cookies," Nilly said, waving the empty package around.

They all sat there in silence; the only sound was Nilly munching away on the last cookie as they tried to think smart and hit-the-nail-on-the-head kinds of thoughts. And, as we all know, it's not that easy to do that on command. Finally there was total silence in Gregory Galvanius's living room. It was so quiet they could hear the faint buzzing sound of the insects in the bedroom; the distant sounds of choral singing from the neighbouring houses, where everyone was glued to their TV sets; and a lone car driving by outside.

Something occurred to Lisa. "I know!" she exclaimed.

Everyone else looked at her.

"I know how people are being hypnotised!"

How People Are Being Hypnotised. And Two Windows Get Broken.

NILLY'S MOTHER AND sister were howling at the top of their lungs. They had forgotten Nilly was missing, because Hallvard Tenorsen was there. On TV. He was conducting with a broad, gleaming white smile, and they were following his baton with their eyes and doing whatever it said. They were in the middle of the second verse of "Norway in Red, White and Blue," a patriotic song that had become popular during World War II when Norway was under occupation by Nazi Germany. They were also nearing the end of their third bag of Cheetos when there was a sudden tinkling sound of breaking glass.

And since it was so late in the evening and they were at home in the safety of their own living room, Eva and her mother jumped like crazy. They stared at the large ice-covered snowball lying on the living room floor surrounded by shards of glass from the smashed windowpane.

"Nilly, you gnomified nitwit!" his mother screamed in rage at the hole in the windowpane. "Have you started vandalising windows now too?"

In response, another ice snowball arrived, smashing the rest of the windowpane.

Nilly's mother and Eva stood up and staggered over

to the window. And there, on the other side of the picket fence, they saw six figures.

"Who's out there?" Nilly's mother yelled.

"The Norway Youth," cried a voice that Nilly's mother recognised right away.

"Truls and Trym Thrane!" she screamed. "Your mother's going to hear about this in an Oslo minute, you catch my drift?!"

"Send that dwarf out here!" Trym yelled back. "Vee want Nilly! Otherwise vee'll break the rest of your windows! This is a presidential recommendation!"

Nilly's mother gave Eva a questioning look, but Eva just shrugged.

"What do you want with Nilly?" his mother yelled.

"Vee're just supposed to bring him to the president, Mrs Nilly!" a high voice called.

"Jeez," Eva told her mother. "That's Beatrize's voice.

I didn't think she was into breaking windows and stuff like that."

"What does the president want with Nilly?" Nilly's mother howled.

"Weren't you listening to the president's speesh earlier this evening, Mrs Nilly? Everyone who's really small or really good at spelling has to meet with the president."

"Why?" Eva yelled at the window.

"Because, as the eighteenth century drinking song that kind of became our first national anthem says, we're the Birthplace of Shampions, which means no one has any business being small here. I'm sure you'll get him back after the president has had a serious shat with him."

"And what about the stuff about spelling?"

"The president doesn't want a bunsh of pesky, uppity spelling know-it-alls picking on people who occasionally forget to double a letter. Seriously, Mrs Nilly!"

Nilly's mother contemplated this. Then she yelled back: "Sounds quite reasonable, all that. And Nilly is lazy, and I'd be more than happy to hand him over to you, tied up if you wanted. But you'll have to tell the president that unfortunately Nilly isn't home."

"Oh well," Beatrize yelled. "So sorry about the broken window, Mrs Nilly, but vee were told that was the way it had to be done. Vee'll just come back later."

Eva and her mother went back to the TV, in time to sing along with the last verse. "Confounded tarnation! Nilly's going to have to pay for that out of his allowance," her mother said, and shivered.

"Nilly doesn't get an allowance, Mum," Eva said, and hurriedly devoured the last of the Cheetos.

NILLY, DOCTOR PROCTOR and Gregory were all sitting around Gregory's coffee table looking eagerly at Lisa. They were looking at her eagerly because she had just said, "I know how people are being hypnotised!"

"You asked what we have in common, those of us who haven't been hypnotised?" Lisa began.

"Yes," Doctor Proctor said. "If we knew that we could figure out how it's happening."

"It's been right there the whole time," Lisa said. "Right in front of our eyes. We just haven't been watching it happening. For whatever reason. And a good thing, too."

"What is she talking about?" Gregory whispered to Doctor Proctor.

"Shh!" Doctor Proctor said.

"But everyone else has been watching," Lisa continued. "My mum and dad. Nilly's mother and sister, Beatrize, Trym, Truls. Everyone in Norway!"

"Of course, it's obvious!" Nilly said, slapping himself on the forehead.

"Eureka!" Doctor Proctor lit up. "That's what we have in common! We haven't been watching!"

"Uh, watching what?" Gregory cried, agitated.

Lisa and Nilly and Doctor Proctor responded in unison: "The NoroVision Choral Throwdown!"

"I wasn't watching because I was doing my homework and practising for band," Lisa said.

"I wasn't watching because I was reading about horrible animals and putting on shadow-puppet shows," Nilly said.

"I wasn't watching because my antenna hasn't been working," Doctor Proctor said.

"And you, Gregory," Lisa said. "You weren't watching because you don't have a TV."

ON THE TV screen at Lisa's house, Tenorsen was on the seventh verse of "Norway in Red, White and Blue" when the glass in the front windowpane shattered.

Lisa's commandant father stared in astonishment at the shards of glass, the shattered flowerpot and the snowball that were lying on the floor in front of his wingback chair. First Lisa had disappeared and now this!

"My lord, what's going on?" Lisa's commandant mother said.

A voice from outside on the street yelled: "Send Flatu-Lisa out here!"

Lisa's commandant father walked over to the window.

"What kind of hooliganism is this?" he roared. "What did you just say about my daughter?"

"She's a very good speller!"

"Of course she's a good speller! And now I'm going to show you how good I am at slapping disobedient shildren upside their heads!"

And with that the large man came trundling out of his living room and started bellowing a ghastly roar that lasted down the front hallway, out the front door, down the walkway, through the gate and out onto the street where the Norway Youth had already long since fled in panic.

Lisa's commandant father stopped there, gasped for breath and mumbled to himself, "But where *is* she?"

"IT'S HALLVARD TENORSEN," Lisa said. "The singing chiropractor. He's hypnotising everyone."

"He's no more a chiropractor than I'm a moon chameleon," Nilly said.

"This is terrible," Doctor Proctor said. "We have a man-eating moon chameleon for a president. And he's planning to start a war against Denmark!"

In silence, they contemplated this grim, deplorable fact for a few minutes.

"All right, all right," Lisa said. "I think we'd better come up with our plan a little faster than this. I have to go home soon and do my homework."

HER COMMANDANT FATHER was standing on the front stoop waiting when Lisa got home.

"There you are! Finally."

He crossed his arms and tried to hide his relief with a gruff expression. "Do you have any idea how worried your mother has been about you?"

"Yes," she said, knowing that her father must have been at least equally worried. "But I had a good reason for being late, Dad."

"Oh yeah? And that reason would be . . ."

"I can't tell either you or Mum. You're just going to have to trust me, Dad."

Lisa's commandant father watched dumbfounded as she marched right past him, into the house and up to the second floor. Her commandant mother came to join him out on the front stoop and asked, "Well, what did she say?"

"That vee have to trust her."

Lisa's commandant mother looked at Lisa's commandant father puzzled. Then Lisa's father put his arm around Lisa's mother's shoulders and cleared his throat. "I have the felling that our little girl isn't so little anymore, honey."

WHEN NILLY GOT home, his house was dark.

Nilly opened his sister's bedroom door a crack and peeked into his mother's room to make sure neither of them had been eaten by moon chameleons yet. But they were both sleeping – at least judging from the snoring sounds – unconcerned and safe. He was about to close his mother's bedroom door when he heard her voice.

"There you are, you slacker. I'm too tired now, but remind me that I'm supposed to tie you up and hand you over to the Norway Youth first thing tomorrow. Okay?"

"Okay, Mum."

"But not until you've brought me breakfast in bed!"

"Of course. Sleep well."

"Humph."

AND THE LAST thing that happened that night was that Nilly put on a short shadow play for Lisa. Not a scary one, because there'd already been enough scary things for one day. It was the longest ski jump in the world, a graceful arc that lasted and lasted, until the ski jumper turned into a bird that, on broad, safe wings, sailed under the moon, into the night and on to the land of dreams, and didn't land until long after both Lisa and Nilly had fallen asleep.

Super-Bait and
Kick-Sledding

SYVERTSEN'S PASTRIES IS in the middle of
downtown Oslo, right next to the parliament building,
three clothing stores, a hair salon and a Freemason's
lodge. Pretentious women from pretentious neighbourhoods sit around its small, round tables on round, slender
chairs. They take demure little tiny bites of baked goods

named after European cities like Berlin, Vienna and Paris, and sip from little tiny cups of tea from remote places in Asia, while they talk about big children and little grandchildren and little tiny goings-on that are happening in their neighbourhoods. But on this day three of them were discussing slightly bigger issues.

"Have you heard? The king has gone into exile abroad," one of them said.

"Yes, to South Trøndelag," another said.

"South Trøndelag is supposed to be very nice," the third said.

"Tenorsen moved into the Royal Palace," the second one said.

"Well, that makes sense," the first said. "He is the president."

"It is rather unfortunate that he declared war on Denmark, though," said the third. "My husband and I, vee had cruise tickets for a little vacation to Denmark, and now of course nothing will come of it."

"Don't say such things," the first said. "Our president knows what he's doing."

But the three ladies weren't the only ones discussing important matters in Syvertsen's Pastries that day. Four people, seated around a table in the very back of the establishment, were discussing nothing short of the end of the world, man-eating moon chameleons and sock thievery. The four people were none other than Doctor Proctor, Lisa, Nilly and Gregory Galvanius. Three days had passed since Lisa and Nilly had outed Gregory as a frog man.

"Do you think she's – *hiccup!* – coming?" Gregory asked, looking at his watch.

"Of course she's coming," Nilly said.

And no sooner had he said that than the door opened. In walked a buxom woman, who purposefully and confidently strode over to their table. She stopped, let her glasses slide down to the tip of her nose, scrutinised the four of them, and asked, "And the four of you are going to save the world from certain doom?"

"There'll be one more of us, Mrs Strobe," Lisa said.

"Oh?" Mrs Strobe replied. "I'm not impressed. And, I must say, this is a rather unusual place for a resistance movement to meet."

"That's exactly the point, Mrs Strobe," Nilly said. "If we'd met at any of the usual resistance movement places, we would have been detected right away."

"We're not forcing anyone to join us, Mrs Strobe," Doctor Proctor said. "After all, being part of this movement entails a not inconsiderable risk."

She stared unflappably at the professor. "I've considered everything you told me," she said. "And I think you're right. Almost all my students developed speech impediments overnight, socks are disappearing left and right and now apparently we're going to be invading Denmark. Something is very wrong." She set her purse down in the middle of the table. "I'm in. Could someone get me a cup of tea?"

Gregory leaped up. His face was flushed and he gallantly pulled one of the unused chairs out for her. "Wonder – *hiccup!* – ful!"

Mrs Strobe raised an eyebrow and gave her colleague a gracious nod. "I think you mentioned there would be one more?"

"He should've been here by now," Nilly said, looking at his watch.

Just then the little bell above the door jingled. They turned and looked at the man who walked in. His polyester pants were so tight he could hardly bend his knees, and his aviator sunglasses were so dark he was about to walk right into the waitress who sailed past him with a tray full of teapots and cups. The man stood there over by the door, waiting for his eyes to adjust to the dim lighting.

"So you invited Band Conductor Madsen," Mrs Strobe said. "How do you suppose he managed to avoid being hypnotised, unlike all the others?"

"Simple," Nilly said, waving to Mr Madsen. "Mr Madsen can't stand choral music. I guarantee he hasn't watched a second of the NoroVision Choral Throwdown."

The man by the door finally noticed Nilly waving and hurried over to their table. He fumbled his way over to the available chair, but didn't sit down.

"Sorry I'm late, but the buses aren't running anymore. They're melting them down to make cannonballs, you know."

"Glad you could make it anyway," Doctor Proctor said.

"That's just it," Mr Madsen said, fiddling with his sunglasses. "I . . . uh . . . can't." Then he sniffled loudly and held out a white slip of paper. Mrs Strobe grabbed it and read it out loud: "'Unfortunately, Mr Madsen has a cold and will not be able to participate in the resistance movement today. Sincerely, Mr Madsen's mother.'"

"Hm," Doctor Proctor said. "That's too bad. What about tomorrow?"

Mr Madsen shook his head.

"The next day maybe?"

Mr Madsen gave a little cough. "It's really quite a bad cold," he said, staring at the floor.

Doctor Proctor sighed. "I see. Then I suppose we'd better just say 'get well soon.'"

"Thank you," Mr Madsen whispered almost inaudibly, taking his note back. And in rapid, mincing steps he shuffled back to the door and left the same way he had entered.

"Well, then I guess that makes five of us," Doctor Proctor said, trying to smile encouragingly.

"The fewer cooks in the kitchen, the less mess," Mrs Strobe said. "What's the plan?"

"The first thing we have to do is find out where the moon chameleons are living, and then we can find out what their plans are," Doctor Proctor said. "And Lisa had a brilliant idea."

"Which is?"

"We set out some kind of bait," Lisa said.

"And use this," Doctor Proctor said. He held up a yellowed cardboard box labelled in all caps: FD&C E18. COLOURING. NOT FOR INTERNAL CONSUMPTION.

"Hey!" Gregory snarled. "That's the stuff that made your strength tonic look like orange juice! That stuff is dangerous!"

"Calm down, Gregory," Doctor Proctor said. "I had a little left in the cellar."

"Ah, I get it. That stuff might kill the moon chameleons," Mrs Strobe said. "But how are we going to get them to eat it?"

"Oh, they're not going to eat it," Lisa said.

"Well, then what . . ."

"Wait and see tonight." Lisa smiled, winking knowingly.

"Ho ho ho!" Nilly cheered. "I'm looking forward to it so much my stomach hurts! Imagine, we're like real guerrilla fighters!" He couldn't sit still anymore and leaped up onto his chair. "We need a name! And – lucky for you guys – I've already come up with one. We'll call ourselves . . ." Nilly paused for effect as he looked around at all the expectant – and some not so expectant – faces. ". . . The Five Vincibles!"

"Uh, you mean the *Invincibles*, don't you?" Mrs Strobe asked.

"The Vincibles, that's a good one!" Gregory laughed. "Ha ha."

"No, I mean *Vincibles*," Nilly said. "That's exactly the point. We can be beaten. We're not indestructible. But we're going to fight anyway. That's what's so great about us!"

They were quiet as they contemplated this. And then one by one they nodded.

"It's a good name," Mrs Strobe said.

"A perfect name," Doctor Proctor said.

"Let's get started," Lisa said.

"Yes, but first we have to celebrate," Nilly said.

"Celebrate what?"

"Having a name. And that we're going to save the world from something super-awful. Tomorrow we may have fallen in heroic battle and then it'll be too late to celebrate."

And after contemplating this for a bit, they all agreed that one heck of a celebration was in order, and Nilly hopped up and down on his chair and waved the waitress over: "More tea, Merete! Tea for the Five Vincibles!"

DARKNESS AND SILENCE had settled over Cannon Avenue.

The houses sat next to each other, quiet and blacked out, but if you listened extra carefully, you could hear sounds coming from three of them. The sounds were coming from the red house, the yellow house and the crooked blue one all the way up at the top of the street, and it was the same type of sound from all three. The sound of a washing machine going around and around. But then the sound in the red house stopped. And then in the blue house. And then finally in the yellow house.

Then there were a few moments of absolute silence. Then, from the blue house, there was a scarcely audible creak, like a window being opened. And then right after that the same creak, as if from a window being closed again. Then a torch in a window in the blue house flashed three times. Which received an immediate response of three quick flashes from the yellow house and the red house. Right after that, the front doors of the red and yellow houses cautiously opened and then closed, and Lisa and Nilly dashed over to Doctor Proctor's house, where they slipped inside.

"Down here!" called Doctor Proctor.

They went down to the cellar, where Doctor Proctor and Gregory were leaning over in front of the washing machine.

"One of them has been here!" the professor said. "I heard the basement window open." Then he pointed to the floor with his torch. "And just as we were hoping, it opened the washing machine and helped itself to a pair of socks."

And sure enough: Wet footprints led from the washing machine over to the cellar window, where the latch on the inside was now open. They hurried outside and found the tracks in the deep snow on the outside of the cellar window. They led through the yard, through the gate and out onto the street. On the compact ice, of course, the footprints from the sock thief disappeared. But not the trail. In the glow from the streetlight, at first glance it looked a little like someone had maybe just peed in the snow. But on closer inspection, you could tell that they were footprints. Yellowish ones, sort of orange juice coloured.

"Now that's what you call bait," Nilly whispered. "Sprinkle our socks with colouring that doesn't come out in the wash, put some in each of our washing machines, and then just wait for a moon chameleon to fall for it. You're a genius, Lisa!"

Lisa smiled. She was quite pleased with herself, too. "Now all we have to do is follow the footprints to find out where they live," she said.

Doctor Proctor got out the kick-sled he'd set out in the deep snow on the inside of his front gate in preparation, since they had agreed that it would be wise to use the quietest possible form of transportation.

"Come on," Gregory said, stepping onto the sled runners up by the handles.

Nilly sat down on the seat and shone his torch at

the footprints, while the professor and Lisa climbed onto the runners behind Gregory.

Gregory kicked off with his powerful frog legs.

"Easy there, Gregory," Doctor Proctor said. "Not too fast. We can't let it suspect it's being followed."

Gregory slowed down a little, and they slid forwards, frog kick by frog kick, in and out of the circles of light from the streetlights, soundless apart from the soft song of the runners on the snow. Nilly shone the torch on the path ahead and gave succinct commands whenever they needed to turn left or right.

A snowman stood in one yard, his round, coal black eyes watching in surprise as the overcrowded kick-sled sailed past.

A while later Nilly whispered, "Stop. There are no more tracks."

Gregory stopped pushing the sled, and they stood completely still as they looked around and listened.

"Maybe it camouflaged itself as that tree over there," Nilly whispered.

"Or that doghouse over there," whispered Doctor Proctor.

"Or to look like snow," Lisa whispered. "But why did its footprints disappear?"

"Wait," Gregory said, without bothering to whisper. He climbed off the kick-sled, and the others watched as he walked back the same way they'd come.

After about sixty yards, Gregory stopped and pointed down at the street. "The last footprint is here, right by this manhole cover. It went down into the sewers." The others had all clustered around him. He bent over and lifted the manhole cover.

Nilly aimed his torch down into the pitch-blackness. All they heard was an echo of water dripping.

"What do we do now?" Lisa asked.

"Simple," Nilly said. "We need volunteers. Anyone who wants to go down there and continue the pursuit, raise your hand."

He counted. It didn't take long.

"No volunteers," Nilly said. "Well, then I volunteer to decide who'll go. And I decide that the volunteer will be . . ." Nilly let his index finger wave around in the air before he pointed to himself: "Me!"

"Just you?" Lisa asked. "Don't you think we all ought to go together?"

"Nope," Nilly said. "One little guy splashes a lot less than four people. Besides, I can crawl into even the narrowest sewer pipes. Watch Perry for me."

Nilly raised his hat, got the spider onto his finger, and passed him to Lisa, who cautiously accepted him.

"Nilly, this is untenable," Doctor Proctor said firmly.

"This is tenable," Nilly said, wrapping his long scarf around his neck one extra time and clearing his throat twice before launching into his farewell address:

"My fellow resistors, fear not. Do not let my sacrifice be in vain. Instead, you must continue to fight against this evil menace. If I don't return, please pass my most affectionate greetings on to my hundreds of adoring female admirers. Tell them Nilly said not to cry. Not too much, anyway." Nilly squeezed his thumb and index finger together, pinching his little turned-up, freckled nose shut, and said a nasal "Farewell!" And with that he did a little jump and – *whoosh!* – he disappeared into the black hole.

"He's crazy!" Lisa said.

"There has actually never," Doctor Proctor mumbled, "been any doubt about that."

The sound of a small splash rose from the sewer way down below.

"On the other hand," Proctor said, "he is right that one person of his stature makes less noise than four people. But he could do with someone who knows their way around down there. Or – what are your thoughts on the matter, Gregory?"

Gregory looked up from the hole and stiffened.

"Why . . . why are you looking at me? *Hiccup!*"

"You swim like a frog," Doctor Proctor said. "You can see in the dark, like a frog. And most important of all: You know some people down there who could help us."

"You're being awfully liberal with your use of the term 'people,'" Gregory said. "They're frogs. Frogs aren't actually very smart, and they're not all that helpful either. Not enough to matter. Frogs aren't really all that, to be honest."

"Look," the professor said, pulling a little flask out of his pocket. "I thought you could take a couple of swigs of this if you got into a tight spot."

Gregory took the flask, looked at the label and read aloud: "Doctor Proctor's Strength Tonic with Mexican Thunder Chilies. Medium Hot." He looked at Doctor Proctor in astonishment. "Victor, you want to make me more froggy? This is the poison that ruined my life!"

"I've . . . uh, tweaked it a little, Gregory. There's less rhinoceros frog extract, so there won't be as many side effects."

"No!" Gregory yelled, so red with rage that he looked as if he were fit to burst. He flung the flask at the ground, where it broke.

"Hm," Doctor Proctor said. "Maybe I should reduce the amount of type A Norwegian lemming as well."

"Hello?" Lisa shouted. "While you're up here arguing, Nilly is alone down there, trying to save the world from something really awful."

The two grown-ups – or people who were older than Lisa, at any rate – looked at her.

"What do you think," Lisa asked, leaning closer to Gregory, "the other members of the Five Vincibles will say if they find out you were too chicken to help Nilly with the moon chameleons, Gregory?"

Gregory snorted so that his breath showed in little clouds of steam rushing out of his nose. "I couldn't care less what that band conductor and Mrs—" He stopped suddenly, his face stiffening. *"Hiccup!"*

"Mrs Strobe?" Lisa asked innocently. "You couldn't care less what Mrs *Rosemarie* Strobe thinks?"

Gregory stubbornly looked Lisa in the eye, not backing down. Then a little less stubbornly. Until finally he grumbled an irritated "Okay, okay. I'm going!"

And with that – without any further ado – he, too, disappeared into the manhole.

The Sewer and
a Secret Weapon

NILLY WAS STANDING waist deep in foul-smelling water, shining his torch into the almost impenetrable darkness. His light illuminated the brownish-black water and the inside of the sewer pipe, where the shadows of scurrying rats appeared many times bigger than the rats actually were. At least, Nilly hoped they weren't that big. When he felt a hand on his shoulder, he was so startled he jumped straight up in the air.

"It's me," Gregory said. "Turn off the light."

"Are you insane?" said Nilly. "Without it we won't be able to see for poo." He looked at Gregory, who just stared back at him blankly.

Nilly sighed. "You didn't get it, did you? *Won't be able to see for poo.* Sewer? Poo? Get it? Uh, it was a joke?"

"I can see just fine without light," Gregory said. "Besides, we won't be able to see a moon chameleon anyway, if it's camouflaged. The good thing about darkness is that the moon chameleon won't be able to see us, either."

"Smart," Nilly said, and switched off his torch. He blinked in the darkness. "Are you there?"

"Hold on tight."

Nilly felt two slimy hands grab hold of him, and a

second later Gregory was giving him a piggyback ride. Or a froggyback ride?

Nilly felt a jolt as they kicked off. Then they were gliding noiselessly through the water and the darkness. Nilly closed his eyes. He felt the same way he had on the seat of the kick-sled – like he was flying.

"Hiccup!" A croak came from somewhere in the darkness.

"Hiccup!" Gregory replied. *"Hiccup, hic, hichic?"*

"Hickety-hic."

"Thanks! Uh . . . *hiccup!"*

"What did he say?" Nilly asked.

"It was a she," Gregory replied.

"Cute?"

"Average. She said she'd heard something splashing up this way, but she hadn't seen anything. Which is really weird since . . ."

"Frogs see super-well," Nilly said.

They continued their swimming tour, and Gregory

kept asking frogs they encountered about the mysterious creature that could only be heard but not seen. And
the frogs kept pointing him onwards, ever deeper into
the network of pipes that runs – crisscrossing every
which way – deep underneath downtown Oslo.

Nilly yawned. All this darkness was making him
sleepy.

"So what do your frog friends say about the rumours
of that sixty-foot-long anaconda that's supposed to be
down here?"

"You don't believe that old urban legend, do you?"
Gregory scoffed. "There. This is where the frog ladies
said they heard that creature disappear."

Nilly looked. Gregory had stopped right under a
pipe that led straight up to the surface. And a thin
strip of yellowish light was making the water around
him glisten.

"Where are we?" Nilly asked.

"What do I look like? A GPS?" Gregory snapped.

"Look, there's a ladder. Come on!"

"Are you absolutely sure we ought to — *hiccup!* — risk it?"

"Well, I'm going to, anyway," Nilly said, hopping off Gregory's back and starting to climb. He stopped a few rungs up the ladder. "Aren't you coming?"

Nilly heard some croaks that he could have sworn were swearing. Then he heard Gregory climbing up behind him.

The ladder ended at a manhole cover with small holes in it that let the light seep in. Nilly tried pushing the cover up, but it wouldn't budge.

"Allow me," Gregory said. He climbed past Nilly and flipped the cover off like it was the top of a box of raisins.

Nilly peered cautiously over the edge, ready to let go and fall back into the sewer water way down below if they were attacked. But that turned out not to be necessary. Not yet, at any rate.

They were surrounded on all sides by tall brick walls with large windows, through which he could see glowing crystal chandeliers and lavishly painted ceilings. Flags were hung from each of the four balconies, one on each wall of the building. And from the floodlit cobblestoned interior courtyard square, Nilly could see only one way out: a tall, black gate with wrought iron bars that extended all the way up to the brick wall surrounding it. On the other side, in the flickering light of four torches, he saw two guards in black uniforms with weird hats featuring even weirder-looking tassels.

Gregory poked his head out next to Nilly's.

"Where the — *hiccup!* — heck is this?"

At this point Nilly could, of course, have replied, "What do I look like? An Oslo tour guide?" But he didn't. In part because he actually knew exactly where they were.

"You see those guards over there with the lame tassels on their hats?" Nilly whispered.

Gregory nodded.

"They're Royal Palace guards. This is the Royal Palace."

"You mean . . . ?"

"The moon chameleons have moved into Norway's Royal Palace. And we're on the inside. Don't you see? We're close to president Hallvard Tenorsen!"

"Hiccup!"

"Quick, we have to get inside!" Nilly exclaimed.

"Double hiccup!"

But Nilly was already up out of the manhole, running, staying in the shadow along the palace wall. Then he stopped and looked around. The only door was just inside the gate, but it was light in there and the guards would catch them right away. He studied the windows. They looked very closed, all of them. But what was that sound? Music? A door on one of the balconies was ajar, and a metallic voice could be heard from within: *"Senorita, don't you want to know . . ."*

"The balcony!" Nilly whispered to Gregory, who had grudgingly run over to meet him. "We have to get up there!"

"We do?" Gregory puffed.

"What? Are you tired?" Nilly asked, surprised. "I thought you were a superfrog?"

Gregory slowly blushed and hissed as quietly as he could: "Listen here, you ungrateful little half-pint! I've swum around half of Oslo with you on my back and you're asking me if I'm *tired*? Just how much energy do you think your average superfrog has?"

"I'd expect him to be able to jump up there," Nilly said, pointing to the balcony with the royal standard of Norway hanging off it – a red flag with a yellow ax-wielding heraldic-looking lion in the middle.

"Now you listen to me . . ."

"Just do it! Come on, Gregory, you know you can. You jumped one hundred and fifty feet on the ski slope without even a ramp! I saw you."

"I just suddenly feel so weak. I don't actually under-stand why . . ."

Nilly started chanting, softly and rhythmically under his breath: "Gregory! Gregory! Gregory! . . ."

Gregory sighed deeply. Then he squatted down, bending his knees as far as he could, and kicked off. And sailed up into the air. Sixteen feet up. Without a running start. A new world's record. But exactly a foot and a half shy of the balcony.

He landed and tried again.

Fifteen feet.

He landed and took off again with a desperate grunt.

Fourteen feet.

Then he collapsed in the shadows, exhausted and gasping for breath. He tried to get up, but remained on his back.

Nilly leaned over him. "Is something wrong, Gregory?"

"It's that music!" he spluttered. "It's her!"

"What are you talking about?" Nilly asked.

"That's a BABA song. That's Agnes singing. That's why I can't do anything."

Nilly listened. The voice from the balcony door sounded cold and indifferent, and Nilly recognised the woman's Austrian accent: *"Hum an old tune, Senorita . . ."*

"You have to be able to do something," Nilly said.

"Can't do a thing," Gregory Galvanius whispered weakly, curling up into a ball, trembling like a draining washing machine.

"Hm," Nilly said, mulling things over in his mind, searching and searching for some solution. And then finding one.

"You liked Perry, didn't you?" Nilly asked.

"Yeah . . ."

"Okay. You see that yellow lion on the flag hanging from that balcony up there?" Nilly asked. "Well, that's not a lion. It's a spider. A big, fat, yellow, juicy . . ."

"Butter spider," Gregory said.

"Yes! Yes, it's a butter spider, Gregory! Doesn't it look delicious? Doesn't it make your mouth water?"

"Yes, yes. I see it now. Or am I just hallucinating? I'm so weak, Nilly."

"You're not hallucinating, Gregory. Gregory! Keep your eyes open. Stay with me, Gregory!" Nilly slapped him and Gregory's eyes sprang open again.

"I want you to eat that delicious spider, Gregory! You should catch it and – wait, wait!"

Gregory's mouth was already open, and his red carpet of a tongue was starting to unfurl. Nilly flung both of his arms and legs around Gregory's tongue.

"Now, Gregory! Now!"

And with that, the tongue shot out with Nilly clinging to it. An instant later, the tongue hit the flag and Nilly's head hit the balcony railing behind the flag. Nilly pulled himself up and just managed to get his hands around the railing before he felt the sticky tongue being yanked away from under his feet, which

were suddenly dangling in midair. His ears were ringing and he was seeing stars, but he didn't let go. He fought, straining with all his might, and got a foot up. And then another one. Then he swung himself over the railing and hopped down. After he caught his breath, he snuck over to the balcony door and stood up just enough so that he could peek in the window.

The room was empty.

Unless there were a dozen moon chameleons sitting and standing around in there, camouflaged to look like the desk, chair, bookshelves, globe, rococo sofa, lamp, wallpaper or large portrait of a poodle hanging above the desk.

The music was clearly coming from the adjacent room, whose door was ajar. Nilly heard voices and quiet laughter. Since none of the furniture moved or attacked him, Nilly assumed it probably *was* furniture, and he tiptoed into the room. Just then he heard a voice from the next room loudly and clearly say: "It's cold, Göran."

And a high, squeaky voice: "Yes indeed, master."

A scratching sound, like claws scraping on wood, was coming closer. Nilly hurried over to the desk and crawled underneath.

Just as the door opened.

From where Nilly was sitting, he could only see the legs of whoever had entered. They were covered with light grey hair and ended in a couple of feet that explained the scratching sound. Because two sets of toes with the longest, most unappealing and unkempt toenails Nilly had ever seen were poking through a pair of ratty white tennis socks. The toenails curled around the ends of the toes and scraped against the wood floor as the bowlegged legs maneuvered towards the balcony door with a swaying, side-to-side gait. The door closed with a bang. The toenail-infested creature bent down to slide the bolt at the bottom of the door shut, and when it did that, Nilly saw something that was even uglier than the toenails. Beneath a long, arching tail, he saw a naked, hairy rear end with something in the middle that made the toenails seem beautiful and appetising by comparison. It was a cluster of bulging pink protuberances that could only be one thing: hemorrhoids. External, monster hemorrhoids that could hardly be pleasant to sit on, and that must itch something awful.

The creature named Göran plucked something up from the balcony door threshold and made a series of loud sniffing sounds. Then squeaky, irritated muttering: "Poop! Filthy britches! That cleaning lady ought to be tortured for this!"

Poop? Poop?! Nilly looked down at his own shoes in alarm and discovered a brown, smushed blob caked onto the sole of his shoe. He must have stepped on a turd in the sewer!

There were some more sniffing sounds. Then the sound of the scraping toenails started coming closer.

Nilly held his breath, but the sound moved away. That Göran creature had gone back to the room next door. Nilly exhaled for a long time, shakily. Because he had no doubt. He had just seen something that very few other people had ever seen: a dreaded moon chameleon.

Nilly stood up to leave again. His mission was completed; they had discovered where the moon chameleons were staying! Now it was just a matter of getting out of here safely. But just then he happened to notice something on the desk. Next to a framed picture of a group of funny baboons, there was a thick document. Nilly stopped in his tracks. The front of the document was stamped with large, red letters that read:

TOP SECRET

The stamp went right over the title of the document, which was:

PLANS FOR INVADING DENMARK

(that lousy little country)

AND THE REST OF THE WORLD

A plan written by Göran Clason,

Luftwaffle Colonel. Translated from the Swedish

by Lieutenant Tandoora Hansen.

Nilly knew he ought to make his escape, but this was exactly the type of document that got the juices of a superspy like him flowing, the kind they dreamed of finding, that they could devote a whole lifetime of spy work to without ever finding! Nilly looked at the balcony door. Gregory was waiting for him. Nilly looked down at the document: *TOP SECRET.* He turned the page. And read:

SUMMARY OF THE PLAN

The plan is basically that we will invade Denmark (that

lousy little country!). But the first step (see Chapter 1) is to strike at their very heart and core, where it will hurt them the most. A bomb in the middle of Legoland (that lousy little town!), which will obliterate that whole pointless collection of Lego blocks! After that we'll give the Danes an opportunity to surrender before it gets any worse (see Chapter 2).

Alternative 1: They surrender, agree to become part of Greater Norway, and together we declare war on Iceland (that lousy, even smaller country!) (see Chapter 3).

Alternative 2: It gets worse. We crush those stupid Danes by letting the even stupider Norwegians shoot them to smithereens. We get them to do this by having our beloved father and benefactor, Yodolf Staler, camouflaged as an idiot named Hallvard Tenorsen, deepen their hypnosis through their daily choral singing ritual that takes place right around bedtime, sorry, prime time (see Chapter 4). Soon the Norwegian people (the whole lousy, measly — well, not particularly big, at any rate — population!) will be willing to shoot their own grandmothers if Yodolf orders it! The ones who don't shoot their own grandmothers — or at least a Dane — will end up in the waffle iron (see Chapter 5).

Waffle iron? Nilly thought, quickly flipping ahead to chapter five. It was titled *CHAPTER 5: NEW SECRET WEAPON FOR USE ON THE CIVILIAN POPULATION. WAFFLE IRON (V1).* The waffle iron looked like a regular one. Only it was super-large. It looked big enough to waffle humans.

Nilly kept flipping through and reading. And reading. And he felt the hairs on the back of his neck stand up. Sure, it had said in his grandfather's book that something super-awful would happen when the moon chameleons started making their presence known, but this . . . this wasn't just super-awful. This was tera-giga-mega-awful. This was awful beyond the natural limits of awfulness. So awful that he had to rub his eyes and read it again. And it was just as shocking then as it had been the first time.

Suddenly he heard the voices from the room next door getting louder and scratchy footsteps coming closer. Nilly flung himself back under the desk just as the door swung open.

"Catch him," he heard a strangely familiar voice growl. This was the moon chameleon Göran called "master."

"Don't let that wretched human get away," a woman's voice said.

And then the high-pitched male voice: "Torture! Yes! Inflict pain, I will! I will!"

Then that familiar voice again: "Shut up, Göran."

Nilly curled up. There simply was nowhere to run. And if what he'd just read was true, the fate that awaited him was worse than getting extra homework, or a tongue-lashing. He closed his eyes.

And then opened them again when he felt a stream of cold air and heard the three voices getting a little quieter. Nilly peeked out from under the desk. And there, on the other side of the now open balcony doors, leaning over the railing, he saw three pink rear ends with the most repulsive clusters of hemorrhoids he had seen since . . . well, three minutes ago.

"There he is!" shouted the woman's voice. "Guard, catch that human before he makes it to the manhole cover!"

Nilly heard several voices from the paved courtyard below and a rattling that made him think of chains, sabers and teeth gnashing. And then a clear: *"Hiccup!"* Oh no – they'd found Gregory.

"Take that, you!" the high voice squeaked. "Tighten the knot! More pain! Torture you, I will! I will!"

"Shut up, Göran. Into the waffle iron with him, no funny business. Can you handle that, Tandoora?"

"Aye-aye, General Staler."

The three figures out on the balcony stood up, turned around and walked back into the room. Nilly quickly ducked back into hiding.

"Where were we, Göran?"

"You wanted to skip step one in my plan – bombing Legoland."

"Yeah, no funny business. We'll just invade Denmark matter-of-factly. Next Wednesday. Got it?"

"Aye-aye, General Staler."

After the three had returned to the room next door and shut the door behind them, Nilly could still hear his own breath whooshing in his ears as if he'd just completed a ten-thousand-metre speed skating race on dull skates.

He had just barely managed to catch a glimpse of the face of the moon chameleon with the deep voice. And Nilly knew three things:

1. He had seen the very face of evil.

2. Gregory was in trouble. In tera-giga-mega-trouble.

3. The end of the world was near.

* * *

"DO YOU THINK something might have happened?" Lisa asked, her teeth chattering as she glanced at her watch.

"I really hope not," mumbled Doctor Proctor, who was kneeling next to the manhole cover listening for sounds from the sewer down below.

"What do you think, Perry?" Lisa asked, turning her head to look at her shoulder, where she'd last seen him. But now the seven-legged Peruvian sucking spider was missing too. Then she spotted him. He was on the ground, near the broken glass from the flask that had held Doctor Proctor's strength drink.

Lisa picked him up. "No more disappearing acts tonight, I'll thank you very much," she said, and tucked him safely under her hat.

"You go home and get yourself and Perry tucked in under a warm blanket," Doctor Proctor said. "I'll wait here alone. Okay?"

"I won't hear another word about that," Lisa said.

"I'm staying right here until Nilly gets back."

Doctor Proctor sighed. "But what if he—"

"Don't say it!" Lisa interrupted. "I *know* that Nilly is coming back. Nilly promised me that he always comes back. And even if Nilly doesn't keep absolutely every promise he makes, he always keeps the important ones."

The professor looked at her without saying anything. And Lisa felt something coming to the corner of her eye. Something that occasionally came if she was very tired and a little down.

"There, there," Doctor Proctor said.

"Do you think . . ." Lisa started, feeling tears starting to tug on her vocal cords. "Do you think we'll . . . ever" – she gulped and gulped, but the clump of tears was forcing its way up and out – "see him again?"

Lisa knew she would start bawling if she said his

name, but she took a deep breath anyway. And just then a familiar voice called up from the hole in the street:

"You mean agent Double O One Million, the Chameleon Spy?"

"Nilly!" Lisa and Doctor Proctor shouted in unison.

The Short Chapter

IT WAS MIDMORNING, and the sun was shining. People were sitting on the park benches along Oslo's main drag in their winter coats, with their pale, smiling faces tilted towards the sun, their eyes shut, possibly dreaming of spring and summer. And about the new Greater Norway. But Lisa, Doctor Proctor and Mrs Strobe were sitting in the darkness at the very back of Syvertsen's Pastries, their ears wide open and horrified looks on their faces as they listened:

"Razor-sharp teeth," Nilly whispered, baring his own small and rather normal teeth. "Protruding snout." He stuck out his lower jaw. "And deep-set, black, expressionless eyes below bushy eyebrows. Like this." He pulled his forehead down as far as he could and scowled, almost making Lisa giggle. After all, she'd already heard Nilly's description of the moon chameleon the night before.

"In other words," Nilly whispered with his lower jaw still stuck out. "They look exactly like baboons. But they speak Swedish."

"And that fits with the rumours that the moon chameleons went to Sweden to start a war from there," Doctor Proctor said. "Apparently they tried for years, but the Swedes just wouldn't fight with anyone, something about neutrality. Because Swedes hate arguments and are deathly afraid of having a falling out with anyone, no matter how much you hypnotise them. These moon chameleons must have spent their formative years in Sweden."

"There were three of them. At least. And I recognised one of their voices," Nilly said. "It was Hallvard Tenorsen's voice. He's the one in charge."

Everyone at the table was quiet for a while as they studied Nilly, who was still wearing his baboon expression so that the others could have sufficient opportunity to study it.

"The point," Doctor Proctor said, "is not where the moon chameleons are from or what they look like, although of course that's terrifying enough on its own. What's really terrifying is that they came here to see if their same super-terrifying plan works any better in Norway."

A sound came from under Nilly's hat, like a little hiccup.

"Poor, poor, poor . . ." Mrs Strobe began, and Lisa counted another four "poors" before their teacher (who otherwise was generally known for her strictness and toughness) finally finished with a "Gregory," practically stifled by sobs.

"Yes," Doctor Proctor said. "And poor, poor, poor the whole world. Tell them, Nilly."

"Well," Nilly said, clearing his throat. "They came up with a plan that goes like this: Greater Norway starts a war with Denmark next Wednesday, and then this war will spread via Iceland, Ireland and India to Iran, Istanbul, the Iberian Peninsula and on to Israel, Iraq, Indonesia . . ."

"Uh, give us the short version, would you?" Doctor Proctor asked.

"Okay," Nilly said. "The moon chameleons are going to start a world war and they want as many people to die as possible."

"Wh-wh-why?" Mrs Strobe asked after a pause.

"Because that's what they live off of," Nilly said. "They eat people."

"*Eat* people?"

"Lots of animals do, you know," Nilly said. "Salt-water crocodiles, pythons, polar bears and at least half of the animals in A.Y.W.D.E. We're just protein, you know. Living hamburgers. The point is that in the near future the moon chameleons are going to need a bunch of food. That's why this is all happening right now."

"Why do they need more food now?"

Nilly pointed up towards the moon. "Their relatives up there. The moon is starting to run out of food. So they're all planning to come here, the whole lot of 'em. They're going to stop by for dinner, you might say. And the dinner is going to be us."

"But this is awful!"

"Yup," Nilly said. "But to them it's really just like when we gather the family together and eat a flock of chickens. I mean, we don't think about them as anything other than food."

"Apart from the fact that in this case they are planning to let the food kill each other in a war instead of doing it themselves," Lisa said.

"That's the most practical way," Nilly said.

"And how do they plan to" – Mrs Strobe searched for the right words – "prepare the food?"

"I saw sketches for waffle irons," Nilly said. "Huge waffle irons. More like the kind of thing you might grill . . ."

"Hamburgers on." Doctor Proctor finished his sentence.

"Oh my God!" exclaimed Mrs Strobe. Then whispered so that it was scarcely audible, "Poor Gregory!"

The table was quiet for a long time, and all that could be heard were cars and trolleys going by outside and a radio on which someone was singing about sunshine and springtime and birdsong.

* * *

FOUR OF THE Five Vincibles stood on the bustling pavement, gazing up towards Norway's Royal Palace, as people hurried past them. Nilly turned to Doctor Proctor:

"Why don't you invent a tank that could drive right through those palace walls up there and get Gregory out?"

"Inventing things like that takes time," Doctor Proctor said. "And it's expensive. Do you know how much just the snow tyres alone for a tank like that would cost? Not to mention the fan belt and—"

He was interrupted by Lisa: "It wouldn't be ready by next Wednesday."

"Exactly," Doctor Proctor said. "What we have to do is use the same weapon the moon chameleons are using."

"Which is?" Nilly asked.

"Influence. Yodolf Staler, disguised as Hallvard

Tenorsen, hypnotises people to do and think what he wants, right? We need to get someone to tell the people that what he says isn't true, that there's no reason for us to go to war against Denmark."

"We're going to get a hypnotist?" Nilly asked. "Cool!"

"No, someone everyone will listen to."

"People only want to listen to Tenorsen," Lisa sighed.

"No, there's someone else," Doctor Proctor said.

"I think I know who you're thinking of," Mrs Strobe said, nodding slowly.

"Who? Who is it?" Nilly cried.

Mrs Strobe nodded towards the Royal Palace. "Don't you remember from history class who the Norwegians listened to during the dark days of World War Two?"

"The king!" Lisa said.

"Exactly," Doctor Proctor said. "We have to go to South Trøndelag and convince the king to convince the people to convince themselves not to listen to Yodolf!" Doctor Proctor sniffed the air. "And time is of the essence!"

Lisa sniffed as well. And of course it could just be her imagination, but she thought she smelled waffles.

"And when time is of the essence that means one thing," Doctor Proctor said. "We'll need to use the MWS."

"The MWS?" Mrs Strobe repeated. "But isn't that . . ."

"The Motorcycle With Sidecar," Doctor Proctor said. "We'll leave for South Trøndelag right away."

"But a motorcycle and a sidecar," Mrs Strobe said, "won't be big enough for all of us."

"You haven't seen this sidecar, Mrs Strobe," Doctor Proctor said. "Come on!"

The Sidecar and the Border Smuggler

IT WASN'T UNTIL Lisa, Nilly, Doctor Proctor and Mrs Strobe had been digging in the snowdrifts in Proctor's front garden for twenty minutes that a pair of motorcycle handlebars finally became visible.

"That'll do," Doctor Proctor said. Then he started digging a cave into the snowdrift, and soon he was totally hidden from view, somewhere in the snow. It was quiet, apart from something that sounded like a hiccup coming from inside Nilly's hat. Three minutes later, they heard a bang from inside the snowdrift. Then another one. Then smoke started seeping out. Then they heard several more bangs that turned into a gurgling engine sound, and then an old motorcycle with the worst-sounding engine anyone has ever heard came smashing out of the snowdrift along with the biggest and most attractive sidecar anyone has ever seen. It was round, like half a pumpkin, was painted gold and had the most elaborate wood carvings. Arranged along the inside were ten red-velvet chairs, enough to seat a whole small orchestra.

"Good Lord!" Mrs Strobe yelled over the noise. "What *is* this?"

"It's a set of box seats from an old theatre!" Doctor Proctor yelled proudly. "I bought the whole box when they were going to demolish Das Goethe Volkstheatre in Leipzig. They threw the chairs in for free."

"Well, there's room for a whole little orchestra in here!" shouted Mrs Strobe. "But what a racket!"

"That's not a racket," Nilly said, smacking his lips in reverie, his eyes closed. "That's a perfect A major. That's a truly musical motor."

"East German motor, Mexican body!" Doctor Proctor yelled over the shrill cackling of the two cylinders. He pulled a bunch of swim goggles out of the panniers. "Put these on and hop aboard!"

"I'm in!" cried Nilly, who had already hopped.

And when everyone was seated, each with his or her swim goggles in place – making the world appear a little yellower, bluer or redder than it actually was – Doctor Proctor turned the throttle grip on his handlebar. And with that they sped away, leaving a whirl of snow behind them.

Someone yelled, "Yippi-yai-yeah!"

You probably know who.

* * *

THEY DROVE AND drove, out of the Oslo metropolitan area, north through a small town and then through an even smaller town, and had just passed a tiny village when they suddenly encountered a sign that said CUSTOMS. Which was odd, because no matter what anyone said, South Trøndelag was not actually another country, just one of Norway's nineteen counties. And then a second sign that said CUSTOIMS, which was odder, because although that was how it sounded when the yokels from the little mountain villages up in these parts pronounced the word, no one ever spelled it that way.

"That means we've reached the border crossing into South Trøndelag!" Doctor Proctor yelled, turning to look at the others who were seated in their velvet upholstered theatre chairs, with their hands tucked in their armpits, singing in three-part harmony to keep warm.

"Stop!" Lisa shouted, pointing.

And sure enough, they saw two signs right in front of them that said exactly that: STOP. Two men in uniform waved them to a stop. One had a strong underbite and an orb of curly black hair under his uniform hat. The other had red cheeks, a round face with bulgy fish eyes and, rather precisely, four long strands of hair combed into an S in the middle of his forehead.

"Are they South Trøndesians?" Lisa whispered.

"They're wearing Norwegian uniforms, so they're probably Norwegian Trøndesians," Doctor Proctor said. "Let me do the talking, okay?"

Lisa and Mrs Strobe nodded.

Doctor Proctor cleared his throat: "Did you hear that, Nilly?"

Nilly sighed heavily. "All right already. Fine."

Doctor Proctor braked to a stop. The guards came over to them.

"Where do y'all think you're going?" the man with the underbite asked in an extremely thick Trøndesian dialect.

"South Trøndelag," Doctor Proctor said.

"Can't y'all see that the border is closed," said the guard with the fish face, pointing to the wooden crossing arm blocking the road ahead of them.

"Ah, yes, we do see that now," said the professor. "What seems to be the problem?"

"We ain't got a problem," said Underbite. "Not if y'all aren't trying to sneak out of Norway and into South Trøndelag, that is."

"And if y'all was, y'all'd be the ones having the problem, not us," said Fish Face.

"Nicely put, you Trønder-rascal, you," said Underbite.

"Thanks, Trønderface," said Fish Face, moving his legs slightly further apart and hooking his thumbs through his belt loops.

"Um, what do you guys mean?" Doctor Proctor asked, pushing up his swim goggles.

"Haven't y'all heard?" Fish Face asked. "President Tenorsen decided that any travel outside of Norway is now strictly off-limits. Anyone who tries to leave will be sentenced for treason and have to face the death penalty. Possibly decapitation."

"If not worse," Underbite said. "And if y'all get ahold of someone in the resistance movement to smuggle you into South Trøndelag, the penalty for that is death."

"If not worse," Fish Face said.

"And where would we find a member of this resistance movement who might do this for us?" Doctor Proctor asked.

"Third forest service road to the right of that spruce tree over there. Red house with a green mailbox. Tell him we said hi and that he'll be getting the death sentence as well."

"We sure will," Doctor Proctor said, turning his motorcycle around and gunning it so the snow flew.

"That was some sidecar, huh," said Underbite, wiping the snow off his underbite.

"Must've been room in there for a whole little orchestra," Fish Face said, wiping the snow off his fish face.

"Looks like they turned onto the third forest service road on the right," Underbite said.

"Just as expected, you Trønder-rascal, you."

THE BORDER SMUGGLER'S name was Guksi, and he was so old his face looked like a stack of pancakes it was so wrinkly. And his ancient body creaked loud and clear as he trudged through the snow, escorting them into the woods. After Doctor Proctor and Guksi had agreed on a price, they'd parked the motorcycle in his barn and set off immediately on foot.

"It was very nice of you to escort us over into South Trøndelag, Mr Guksi," Doctor Proctor said.

"Shut up," Guksi whispered. He spat in the snow and glanced up at the high-voltage lines running up above the treetops. "We need to be quiet. This isn't without its danger, this border smuggling business, you know. If they spot us, they'll shoot us."

"Good Lord," whispered Mrs Strobe. "Wh-wh-who will?"

"The South Trøndesians. Sh!"

They stopped suddenly, holding their breath while Guksi put a hand behind his ear.

A sound came from deep within the forest: *cuckoo, cuckoo.*

"A cuckoo bird," Lisa whispered.

"Sounds South Trøndesian, doesn't it?" Guksi said.

They listened again.

Cuckoo, cuckoo.

"To me it sounds exactly the same as a Norwegian cuckoo bird," Lisa whispered.

"Well, to the untrained ear, perhaps," Guksi said. "But those of us with special innate abilities can hear the difference. Come on, we're on the right path."

He straightened up and kept walking, his legs and joints creaking and groaning as he tottered along.

"What kind of innate abilities do you actually have?" Nilly asked.

"Oh," Guksi said. "A little of this, a little of that. A bit of clairvoyance that allows us to see what's going to happen. Hands that can cure all kinds of ailments. Arthritis that warns me about everything from nice weather with a few clouds to avalanche risk. Nothing special, really."

"So what do you see now?" Lisa asked.

"I see . . ." Guksi squeezed his eyes shut. "I see . . . that the sun is going to rise at exactly seven fifty three tomorrow morning. And I see that you're going to meet someone soon who will be significant in your future."

"That must be the king!" Lisa exclaimed.

"There! You see? I have the gift," Guksi said, satisfied.

"What do you think about the end of the world?" Nilly asked. "Have you seen any signs of it coming lately?"

"Oh, the end of the world comes and goes," Guksi said. "That's South Trøndelag for you."

They had emerged from the forest, and ahead of them lay open countryside. And it was obvious to all of them that it was South Trøndelag, because in front of them there was a river, and on the other side of the river there was a road, and next to the road under the high-voltage line there was a house, and next to the house there was a banner, and on the banner it said:

SOUTH TRØNDELAG'S

LARGEST HANG GLIDER SELECTION.

BUY NOW!

(SEE HOW FAR THE PRICE HAS BEEN

MARKED DOWN?)

"Good," Doctor Proctor said. "But how do we get across this?"

He pointed at the river, which was unusually wide, greenish black and most definitely both icy cold and deep. And there was no bridge in sight for as far as the eye could see, either downstream or upstream.

"Afraid I can't help you there," Guksi said, picking his nose so that his nostril creaked.

"But my dear sir," Mrs Strobe said. "We did pay you to escort us to South Trøndelag."

"Yup, and now I've shown you the way. I mean, it's not that hard. All you have to do is follow the high-voltage lines."

They looked at the high-voltage lines running over the river to the next pole and then disappearing off into the Republic of South Trøndelag. And, of course, there was a rowboat with oars in it sitting on the riverbank on the South Trøndelag side, just to taunt them for being on the wrong bank.

"Don't despair," Guksi said. "Because I'd be happy to guide you back to your motorcycle for half the price you paid me to bring you here."

"No thank you!" all four Vincibles said, pretty much in unison.

"No? Well," Guksi said, "good luck with that, then."

Then he turned around and walked back into the woods the same way they'd come.

"NOW WHAT DO we do?" Mrs Strobe sighed. They had sat down in the snow, gazing across at the other side of the river.

"Maybe we can swim across," Lisa suggested.

Doctor Proctor shook his head. "The current is too strong, and the water is too cold. We'll have to follow the high-voltage line back to Guksi's. What are you doing, Nilly?"

"Looking for . . . ," Nilly mumbled with his head down in his tiny backpack, "these!"

He came back up with a triumphant grin, holding a pair of red and orange shoes in the air.

"Hey!" Doctor Proctor said sharply. "Those are my balancing shoes!"

"I brought them along," Nilly said. "Thought maybe we might have a use for them."

He started putting them on while the other three watched him blankly, not understanding what he was doing. Then it seemed to dawn on two of them. Lisa saw Doctor Proctor turn and look up at the high-voltage lines that stretched across the river.

"No . . ." Lisa began.

"You . . . you can't be serious . . ." Doctor Proctor said.

"You're planning to . . . planning to . . . ," Lisa said.

"Excuse me, but what are you talking about?" Mrs Strobe asked. "And what do those weird boxing shoes have to do with all this?"

"These," Nilly said, "are Doctor Proctor's Balancing Shoes. And these shoes are going to get me across the river so I can row that boat over here."

"In that case, I'll have to be the one to do it," Doctor Proctor said.

Nilly licked his index finger and was now holding it up in the air. "Do you feel that? The wind is picking up. Which means that tall people would be blown right off the wires. What we need here is a little guy. Preferably one with red hair."

"Hm," the professor said, studying the treetops. And, sure enough, they were really swaying around.

"It *could* work," Lisa said.

Mrs Strobe looked at the professor, looked at Lisa, looked at Nilly, and then looked up at the high-voltage lines.

"I think," she said slowly, "that you three are stark raving bonkers, totally unhinged and completely insane."

"There has actually . . ." Doctor Proctor smiled.

". . . never been . . ." Lisa laughed.

". . . any doubt about that!" Nilly completed the sentence.

Line Dancing and a Trøndesian Named Petter

THE WIND ROARED in Nilly's ears. His lips were pursed in deep concentration, his arms stretching out to his sides. He was looking straight ahead while putting one foot in front of the other with the utmost caution. A gust almost sent him toppling head over heels off to the side, but the shoes sort of suctioned a firm hold on the metal wire beneath him.

As he regained his balance, his hat made a little jump on his head.

"Stop hiccuping, Perry!" Nilly whispered. "I'm trying to concentrate here!"

He glanced down.

"And don't look down, Nilly!" he quickly whispered to himself, bringing his eyes back up again.

But it was too late. He had already seen how dizzyingly far it was to the surface of the water below him. Which was also black. Black as asphalt. And probably just as hard, at least if you came plummeting down from a height of several hundred feet. Nilly remembered his grandfather's story about the time when he was a sailor and went ashore in San Francisco along with the third mate and it was so hot they decided to go for a swim and they jumped off the Golden Gate Bridge. But they only had one pair of swimming trunks; they were blue and quite loose fitting. So they had played rock-paper-scissors for the swimming trunks and his grandfather had done rock and the third mate had done paper, and this was back when paper beat rock. So the third mate had triumphantly removed his third mate's hat, pulled on the loose swimming trunks, climbed up over the railing and jumped. And Nilly's grandfather had watched, watched the third mate getting smaller and smaller, and realised that they were much higher up than it had appeared. And when the third mate hit the water, Nilly's grandfather realised that the surface was much harder than one might have thought. Basically, it was good-bye to the third mate. All that was left were the blue, somewhat loose swimming trunks, which floated back up again. And Nilly had often wondered, What if his grandfather hadn't chosen paper that time, what if he had been the one to jump, and then he never would have met Nilly's grandmother and had his Dad so that Nilly could be born. Although right now Nilly was wondering if that actually would have mattered anyway. Because another gust of wind came and grabbed hold of the high-voltage lines. It made Nilly sway so violently that for a second he was looking straight down at the black water, which now had a fair number of teeny tiny whitecaps on it.

Nilly bent his knees, struggled to keep his balance, and waited for the wire to stop swaying. But there was still a long way to go to the other side, and the wind wasn't letting up. He couldn't quite see how he was going to be able to do it, with or without the balancing shoes. But he had to. It was as simple as that. So he put his left foot in front of his right. Then his right in front of his left. It wasn't going so badly. Had the wind died down a little? Yes, it had. Nilly heard a voice shout something from a distance. It was Lisa from back behind him, down by the shore. But he didn't want to turn around. He wanted to hurry. He moved his feet faster. Then even a little faster.

Well, there was absolutely no wind now. Maybe this was going to work after all? And that's when he heard it. A rushing, roaring sound from the forest. And out of the corner of his eye he could see the tops of the enormous spruce trees down below him along the riverbank. They were pitching to and fro, leaning over sideways in the colossal gusts of wind. And Nilly knew that he was lost. It was as if the wind had just been inhaling, gathering all its strength to blow this cheeky little redhead down from where he didn't belong. And now it was exhaling at full force. Nilly hunkered down as the initial squall line buffeted him and blew his orange hat off. He saw it fly away, first up a ways, then swirling downwards until it became a small dot. The second gust sent him spinning twice around the high-voltage wire before the third and final gust sent him off into midair.

"Urraaaaaaaaaah!" Nilly screamed and fell.

"Hiccup!" Perry hiccuped.

They slowly turned in the air so that Nilly first saw the high-voltage wire above them getting farther away, and then saw the surface of the water below them getting closer.

"Double urraaaaaaaaah!" Nilly screamed.

"Hiccup-hiccup!" Perry hiccuped.

Because of course they both knew what the outcome would be. Flat as pancakes with strawberry jam.

Nilly closed his eyes.

Kept them shut.

Waited.

And waited.

And waited.

Wasn't the crash going to come soon?

Yes, yes, the longer it took the stronger it would be when it finally happened.

He squeezed his eyes shut even tighter.

Come on now, get it over with!

But, no. Nothing.

How high could they have been? Because this was actually starting to get a little boring. Or maybe he was already dead?

Nilly cautiously opened one eye. He could still see the river way down below him, but it wasn't getting any closer. The opposite, actually. It looked like it was getting a little farther away. And something around his hips was tugging, as if he were wearing a harness.

Nilly turned to the side and looked up.

And could hardly believe what he saw.

A skinny thread was running straight up from him, apparently into midair. And Perry was sitting on the thread right above him. Slowly it dawned on Nilly what it was: a spiderweb.

"Hello?" Nilly asked. "Am I dreaming?"

"Hiccup!" Perry said.

"Am I hanging from a cobweb? Is that possible, Perry?"

But before he got any response, the wind picked back up again and caused them to swing back and forth as if they were sitting on an enormous swing right over the river. And the cobweb held! Nilly sat there feeling quite pleased about his life. Until he realised that the world was about to end anyway. He had to act. He had no idea how a cobweb from a completely average seven-legged Peruvian sucking spider could hold a guy with so much muscle mass and an oversized brain, but he could think about that later.

"Perry!" Nilly yelled. "Can you make the thread even longer?"

And Perry could. Soon they were hanging right over the surface of the river, and Nilly stretched his small legs straight out and leaned back in his cobweb harness. They swung a little forward. He leaned forwards and bent his knees under him. They swung backwards. He stuck his legs straight out and repeated his pumping action. Their speed slowly increased, and the arc they were swinging in got bigger and bigger. In the middle of the arc, Nilly's feet almost dragged through the water while over on the sides it was a long way down, the air rushing past his ears. And then there was a puff of wind from behind, and the swing with Nilly and Perry on it swung all the way over the far bank.

"Let her rip!" Nilly yelled.

And with that, Perry unfurled even more cobweb and Nilly sank down onto the ground.

"Yippee!" Nilly shouted as he landed gently in the snow on the riverbank. He tugged on the thread.

Perry must have bit it off, because the end soon

drifted down. Nilly ran over to the rowboat, pushed it out, jumped in and snapped the oars into the oarlocks. As he rowed, he spotted Perry sitting on the seat in front of him.

"Ingenious!" Doctor Proctor yelled as the boat reached him and he helped the others aboard.

"Fantastic," Mrs Strobe said, pinching Nilly's cheek.

"But what actually happened?" Lisa asked after she gave Nilly a hug.

"My hat blew off and we fell," Nilly said, leaving the rowing to Doctor Proctor and Mrs Strobe, who had each grabbed an oar. "It's really unbelievable, but Perry must have shot out a thread of cobweb around the high-voltage line and then attached the other end around me. It was like falling attached to a rubber band; I didn't even notice that we'd stopped. But I don't really understand how that's possible."

"Hiccup!" Perry said.

"Hm," Doctor Proctor said. "But I think I do. Do you

remember the flask Gregory smashed on the asphalt? The one containing Doctor Proctor's Strength Tonic with Mexican Thunder Chili, Medium Ho—"

"Yeah, yeah!" Lisa and Nilly yelled impatiently.

"Do you also remember that we picked Perry up off the ground and that he was standing in the middle of those glass shards?"

"Aha," Lisa said.

"Aha," Mrs Strobe said.

"Aha!" Nilly said. "Perry, you sneaky spider! You tasted the strength tonic, didn't you?"

Perry didn't respond.

"With such a small body, it wouldn't take more than a few drops to make him super-strong," the professor said.

"And make him spin super-strong spiderwebs," Nilly said.

"And start hiccuping," Lisa said.

They had crossed the river and pulled the boat up

onto the bank. Then they walked up to the road that ran in front of the house with the big sales banner.

"We could try to hitchhike into South Trøndelag proper," Doctor Proctor said.

"Or maybe a bus will come along soon," Lisa said.

They stood there for a while looking up and down the road, but no one came: no cars, buses, motorcycles with sidecars, kick-sleds or anything else.

"Seems pretty deserted," Nilly said.

"Maybe someone in the shop can help us," Doctor Proctor said.

THE SHOP TURNED out not to be a normal shop, but more of a large hall. They walked over to a very empty, very deserted counter.

"Hello?" Doctor Proctor called out, but the only response was an echo.

"What's that?" Lisa asked, nodding at the strange devices scattered across the floor. They were the size of trampolines and consisted of colourful sailcloth stretched over frames, with a bunch of attached bars and strings. Underneath each sailcloth frame, there was something that looked like a sleeping bag.

"It looks like someone didn't read the instructions for how to set up their tent," Nilly said.

"Those are hang gliders," Doctor Proctor said. "If you take one of these high up in the mountains, you can get a running start, take off, and then just lie down in this sack under the wings as you fly away. For hundreds of miles if you luck out in terms of the wind and weather conditions. HELLO?"

"HELLO!" Nilly shouted.

Nothing happened.

"There doesn't seem to be anyone here," Lisa said.

Just then there was a bang that made the air in the hall vibrate.

"Wh-wh-what was that?" Doctor Proctor asked.

Nilly nodded at Mrs Strobe's hand, which was still resting on the counter.

"Mrs Strobe's signature move," he whispered. "Hand slap on the teacher's desk."

"Could you ask her not to do that again?" Doctor Proctor said, stretching his jaw and shaking his head to try to get his ears to pop.

They heard rattling from somewhere, a door opened, and in came a young man in a tight red leotard with black oil stains on the outside of it and a teeny tiny little potbelly on the inside. He looked liked he'd just rolled out of bed, because his blond, bushy hair was sticking up in all directions, and from behind the thickest eyeglass lenses Lisa had ever seen, a pair of narrow eyes peered at them.

"Flabbergast me!" he said with a mixture of fear and excitement. "There's people here! No one's been in here since last Easter!"

"Hello, Mr . . ."

"Petter! I'm Petter! I'm the one and only Petter and a heck of a Petter I am!"

"I see. I'm Doctor Proctor, and this is Lisa, Nilly and Mrs Strobe."

Petter leaned over and took a closer look at Nilly. "Are you sure your name's not Petter, son?"

"Quite sure," Nilly said.

"You look like a Petter."

Nilly shrugged. "You're the only Petter here, Petter."

"And you can bet your moonshine on that!" Petter said, straightening back up again. "What are you folks doing here?"

"We came to find the king," Lisa said. "The king of Norway, that is."

"He has a cabin in the big city," Petter said.

"The big city?"

"Klæbu, population three thousand and sixty-three.

It's far from here, though. Sixty miles. Do y'all have a car?"

"No," Lisa said. "But maybe there's a bus?"

Petter shook his head. "Everyone moved to Norway. Or Klæbu. I'm the only one left." He stretched his arms out to either side, tilted his head back and yelled: "I'm Petter! Petter! Ain't nobody better!"

"Um, do you have a car, Petter?" Doctor Proctor asked. "We would gladly pay you for a lift into Klæbu."

Petter shook his head and adjusted his eyeglasses. "Near-sighted. Quite bad. Those cowards at the DMV wouldn't give me a driver's license. That's why I never make it to Klæbu. I'll never make it out of this hole without a driver's license." He tipped his head back and screamed at the ceiling again. "Cowards! I'm Petter, come on!" He stopped abruptly and looked at them. "I suppose they were afraid I'd run somebody over. But now that every last person can just drive wherever they want, there are no pedestrians left to run over. Why can't I get a driver's license? Why is everyone against me?"

"What about your boat?" Lisa said. "Could we borrow it?"

Petter shrugged. "Klæbu is upstream from here. And the other direction, the river is all waterfalls and rapids."

The Four Vincibles gave each other dejected looks.

Then suddenly Petter lit up: "Wait! I have hot chocolate! I did a hot chocolate commercial back in my hang gliding days, you know. I was good. I beat them all! Child's play! I'm Petter! Should I make you some hot chocolate? I've got a cupboard full!"

"I don't know," Doctor Proctor said, looking at his watch. "The invasion of Denmark is going to start in forty-eight hours."

Petter looked pleadingly at them: "Can't you all just stay for a little while? We could play Chinese checkers. I'm good, you know! I'm Petter!"

"Sorry," said Doctor Proctor.

"Don't go! I'll put whipped cream on the hot chocolate."

Doctor Proctor looked at the other three.

"I think he's a little lonely," Lisa whispered. "I guess we could stick around for a little while."

Doctor Proctor turned to Petter with a big smile: "We'd love to have a little hot chocolate."

LISA AND NILLY helped Petter make the hot chocolate in the small kitchenette over by the one wall.

"I'm going to get out of here someday, you know," Petter said. "If I could only just sell the rest of these hang gliders, I could get out of here. Yes, maybe I'll make it all the way to Oslo and visit you guys. If you'd like a visit, that is."

"We'd love one," Lisa said.

"How are hang glider sales these days anyway, what with no one living out here and all?" Nilly asked.

"Things aren't going well at all," Petter said gloomily. "The sale's been going on for almost three years now, but there are hardly any customers." He lit up. "But maybe I could interest you all in a hang glider?"

Lisa laughed. "I don't really think we need any . . . uh, hang gliders, Petter."

The hope behind those thick eyeglass lenses, correction minus seventeen, faded again. "No, of course not. What would you all do with a hang glider?"

It was quiet for a while in the kitchen as they listened to the rumbling from the saucepan, keeping an eye on the hot chocolate so it wouldn't boil over.

"Although, actually . . ." Nilly said. "I think . . . I *think* I actually have an idea."

Oh no, Lisa thought.

Launch with a Sprinkle of Cinnamon

"HOW DID YOU even think we were going to fly a hang glider to Klæbu?" Doctor Proctor asked, shaking his head. "I mean, to begin with, none of us even knows how to fly a hang glider."

"Petter has a family-size hang glider," said Nilly, who was hopping up and down the way he usually did whenever he thought something fun was about to happen. "And he knows how to fly it. Right, Petter?"

Petter nodded. "Sure, sure. But it only has room for four, and there are five of us."

"Lisa and I will fit in the same sleeping bag," Nilly said. "And Doctor Proctor is just a skinny beanpole. I'm sure there'll be plenty of room."

The professor looked at Petter, who shook his head sadly.

"The launch," Petter said, and Doctor Proctor nodded.

"What?" Nilly asked. "What do you mean?"

Doctor Proctor sighed. "The launch. Taking off. It's great that you're such a creative thinker, Nilly, but look around. Do you see any mountains we can take off from? Well?"

Nilly looked out the window at the flat-as-a-pancake countryside surrounding the hall.

"We could just start *walking* to Klæbu," the professor suggested.

"Oh, but there's still more hot chocolate," Petter said, his voice sounding a little helpless. "I could add a sprinkle of cinnamon on top? And we haven't even started playing Chinese checkers."

Doctor Proctor, Mrs Strobe and Lisa shook their heads, thanked Petter for the hot chocolate, buttoned up their jackets and were about to leave when they heard Nilly's voice exclaim, "I've got it!"

They turned around. Nilly was still sitting at the table, staring down into his empty hot chocolate mug.

"What've you got, Nilly?"

"Pour another round of hot chocolate for everyone, Petter."

Petter lit up. "With a sprinkle of cinnamon on top?"

"Not exactly cinnamon," Nilly said.

"What are you talking about?" Lisa asked.

"I'm talking about a launch," Nilly said.

"ARE YOU SURE this is going to work?" Petter asked. He was bending over, holding on to the control bar of the big family-size hang glider.

"No," said Doctor Proctor, who was lying on his back. "You can still back out if you want."

"No thanks. I'm in," Petter said, gripping the bar harder. "I want to go to Klæbu."

"Good," Doctor Proctor said, raising his hot chocolate mug. "Everyone ready?"

"Ready!" called Lisa and Nilly, who had climbed into the sleeping bag on one side.

"Ready!" called Mrs Strobe, who was lying in the sleeping bag on the other side.

"Then let's drink," Doctor Proctor said.

And with that they all emptied their hot chocolate mugs in one, long gulp.

"Four," Nilly said.

"Mmm," Petter said appreciatively. "Considering that it wasn't cinnamon, it wasn't bad. What did you call the powder again?"

"Doctor Proctor's Fartonaut Powder," the professor said, smacking his lips in satisfaction. "The essence of pear really makes a statement, don't you think?"

"Three," Nilly said.

"And you all really think a powder can get us to Klæbu?"

"Well . . ." Doctor Proctor said.

"Two," Nilly said. "One."

"It's tickling," Petter laughed, rubbing his potbelly.

"Zero," Nilly announced.

Then everything went white.

And after the echo of the bang had reverberated back and forth across the river a couple of times and the snow had settled again, there was nothing left in the yard in front of the hall. Just a pole with a flapping banner announcing South Trøndelag's largest selection of hang gliders. Once again it was quiet, but if you listened carefully, you could just make out a cry from way up in the sky:

"Flabbergast me! I'm Petter! I'm the one and only Petter and a heck of a Petter I am!"

LISA STARED. THE countryside below them looked like a map slowly gliding by. It was even colder up here; she felt it on the tip of her nose. But inside the sleeping bag it was nice and warm.

And it was so quiet! Just the rustling from the large red wing, a soft creaking of the cables tightening and loosening, the ticking of the altimetre as they rose and the nearly inaudible snoring of Nilly, who had fallen asleep beside her.

Every now and then Doctor Proctor said something to Petter and pointed at the map they'd brought from the wall in the hall. And eventually Doctor Proctor

was allowed to steer, while Petter showed him how everything worked.

The sun had sunken down into the sea way out in the west, where the sky gradually changed from blue to orange to red and – at the very bottom – greenish purple. Every now and then they soared over a house with lights shining from its windows, and now and then over a road with its streetlights on, making it look like a glowworm in the gathering twilight.

It was so beautiful that Lisa could only manage to think one thing: that this world was so wonderful, they just had to save it.

An hour later it was dark and Doctor Proctor pointed at the carpet of lights appearing out of nothing below them.

"Klæbu," he said.

But by then Lisa was already asleep.

An Audience and
Morse Code

"YOUR ROYAL HIGHNESS, you have visitors."

"What?" The king looked up from the crossword puzzle he was doing in the *South Trøndelag Times* and glanced at the clock. It was eleven o'clock at night. Visitors now? He looked up at his butler Åke, who was standing before him in the living room doorway. Åke was a tall man who looked like someone had used a pencil sharpener on him. He had a sharp nose, pursed lips, sharp chin, sharp teeth. And a sharp tailcoat that tapered down to two points below his backside. He also rather often made pointed comments about what the king was or was not doing. But he made them in Swedish, so the king didn't always fully understand the nuances of just how pointed they were. The king did occasionally wonder why he had hired Butler Åke, but then he remembered that it was relatively cheap to hire guest workers from Sweden, and besides they seemed to like to work for Norwegians in poorly paid, servantlike jobs. Plus, Butler Åke had shown up at his doorstep asking for a job the very day the king arrived here after that presidential imbecile threw him out of his Royal Palace.

But sometimes the king felt like Butler Åke was laughing at him behind his back. Not that it mattered at a time like this, without access to his royal household resources, living in exile abroad. The king couldn't afford anything other than a cut-rate Swedish man-servant, so he would just have to put up with Butler Åke's snide Swedish comments.

"They landed in a hang glider outside," Åke said. "They say they snuck across the border to speak to Your Royal Highness, and they request an audience. Shall I show them in?"

"Hm," the king said, glancing down at his news-paper. These South Trøndelag crossword puzzles were so darn difficult.

Åke sighed in that irritating, pointed way of his, and then said, "One across, Oona."

The king counted the letters in the crossword and decided it was right. After all, he was the king.

"Let's see," he continued with his finger on the next line. "Six across, five letters. 'If you have this, you have the ability to think rationally.'"

"They're waiting, Your Royalness."

The king had noticed that Butler Åke was more and more prone to shortening his title, and he didn't like it. But he was afraid that if he demanded to be addressed with his full title each time, Butler Åke would ask for a raise.

"Yeah, yeah, send them in, then," the king said, waving his hand in irritation.

Åke ducked out and then came back in, holding the door open. And an unusual group entered. First a skinny beanpole of a man wearing swim goggles, then a teensy-weensy little boy with freckles and red hair with something that looked like an insect sitting in it, then an apparently normal-looking girl with braids. But it was the last person that made the king really open his eyes wide: a voluptuous lady with a strict face and a nose that never seemed to end. She was – pure and simply – one of the most beautiful women the king had ever seen.

"Your Royal Highness," the beanpole in the swim goggles said. "I am Doctor Proctor, and we have come to tell you that you must talk some sense into the Norwegian people."

"That's it!" the king lit up and filled in six across. S-E-N-S-E.

"Does that mean you'll do it?" asked the beanpole, who'd called himself Doctor Something-or-other.

"Well, there's doing and then there's doing," the king said. "I dare say I have enough to do already." He nodded at the three-foot-tall stack of crossword puzzles on the floor next to him.

"Your country needs you, King," the little red-haired boy said. "Otherwise the world is in for a, well, a world of trouble. You have to come back to Norway with us."

"Back? To that president who threw me out?" the king gave a quick, bitter laugh.

"Hallvard Tenorsen must be stopped!" the little girl said. "That's not even his real name. His name is Yodolf Staler and he's a moon chameleon."

"You don't say," the king said. "Uh, a moon chameleon? What's that?"

"They look like baboons and their rear ends are full of hemorrhoids," the boy said.

"Yes, well, whose aren't?" the king mumbled,

scanning his crossword. He had seen a clue that said "monkey" somewhere. Perhaps "baboon" was the answer.

"Tenorsen has the whole population hypnotised," the girl said. "He just looks into the camera and then everyone who looks into his eyes too long develops a weird speech impediment and does exactly what he says."

"I'm not impressed," the king said. "I learned how to hypnotise people when I was crown prince. That's what I do when I give the king's traditional New Year's speech on TV, you know. I hypnotise people to want to keep the monarchy instead of some newfangled president and all that silliness." He looked up from his crossword. "Actually, would you like me to hypnotise you a little right now? *My fellow countrymen . . .*"

"No thank you," said the little girl. "Tenorsen wants to cook Mr Galvanius and invade Denmark next Wednesday. Which is the day after tomorrow. You have to come with us, Your Royal Highness."

"It's out of the question," the king said. "I'm doing splendidly here: satellite TV, no toll roads, cheap gas, no foreigners – well, apart from me and Åke, that is. And South Trøndelag hotdogs are *way* better than . . ."

The next instant, it was like the room exploded. The king jumped right out of his chair and when he landed again, he was staring terror-stricken at the hand that had just slapped the table in front of him. A dreadful, infernal slap that had made his heart stop for a second only to once again start beating at triple the usual pace. The king's eyes slowly moved from the hand up the arm to the shoulder. To the face, to the long nose, to the glasses, to the piercing eyes that looked as if they were staring straight through him.

"Listen up," said the voice, which was at least equally piercing. "You, my boy, are going to help us save the world. Got it?"

"Wh-wh-who are you?" the king managed to stammer.

But there was no answer, just those eyes trained on him, making it impossible for him to look away.

"That's Mrs Strobe," he heard the red-haired boy say. "What you just heard was the Strobe Desk Slap, and what you're seeing now is the Strobe Stare."

"The S-s-strobe Stare?"

"Yup. Can you feel how it's drilling into your brain, which in a few seconds will start bubbling and boiling?"

"L-l-leave my brain alone."

"On one condition," said the woman called Mrs Strobe. "That you do your job as king."

"Exactly. Uh . . . um, which job is that?"

The little girl with the braids took over: "Which is to tell the Norwegian people that Yodolf Staler is a fraud and that they shouldn't be doing what he says. They need to oust him from the presidency. And they need to do it now!"

"Oh dear," said the king. "And you guys think I can accomplish all that just by . . . uh, giving a speech?"

The whole delegation in front of him nodded.

"And that's it?" the king asked. "Give a speech?"

"Yup, that's basically it," the beanpole in the swim goggles said. "Pretty much like your ancestor, King Haakon the Seventh, did from London during World War Two. He spoke to the people, encouraged them to fight in the face of a superior power."

"Hm," the king said. "Did it work? Did they do it?"

"Well, maybe not as much as one might have wanted, but more than if he hadn't said anything at all."

"I see." The king looked at them thoughtfully, weighing the pros and cons. That ancestor of his had given a few short speeches over the radio, so he'd been able to sit right back down in his comfy chair by the fireplace and do his crossword puzzles. And of course, most wonderful of all, he'd been able to move back into the Royal Palace afterward. On the other hand, writing a speech like that was a tremendous amount of work.

"We trust you, Your Royal Highness," Mrs Strobe said gently, smiling at him.

And he simply thought, *Yowzers, she's hot!* Then he leaned in towards her: "Between us, Mrs Strobe, I think all that business about addressing me as Your Royal Highness can get a little stuffy. If you just wanted to call me Your Royalness, that would be fine."

"Oh, thank you so much, Your Royalness," Mrs Strobe said, batting her eyelashes. "And you can call me Rosemarie."

"Heh, heh," said the king.

"So, will you do what we're asking?"

"Well," the king said. "It's late, so let's sleep on it. Åke, make up some princess beds for our guests."

Åke did an about-face. "We only have basic bunk beds."

"What the . . ."

"You're living in a rustic cabin in the mountains, not a palace, Your Royalness."

"Highness, Åke."

"Pardon me?"

"Your Royal High . . . Forget it. Fine, bunk beds, then. And supper." He turned back to Mrs Strobe. "I have hot dogs, Rosemarie. Bought them at Seven-Eleven. Very good, very cheap."

"Oh, thank you, thank you, Your Royalness."

"Heh, heh," the king said.

"And there's one more thing," the red-haired boy said.

"Oh?" the king asked skeptically. Because there was always *just* one more thing. And in general this "just" business was one of the things he liked least.

"You have to ask us to save Gregory," the little boy said. "And the country. And, for that matter, the rest of the world."

"I do?"

"Yes, you do."

"How come?"

"Because you're the king," the boy said. "And if we're going to die, we want it to be for king and country, you know? It makes for good morale, you see?"

The king thought about it. "Okay," he said, scratching his right buttock. "I hereby request that you save Gregorious. And the country. And, for that matter, the rest of the world."

"Yippi-yai-yeah!" the young boy howled.

"Thank you," the girl said, and curtsied.

LISA COULDN'T SLEEP. And it wasn't because she'd eaten way too many South Trøndelag hot dogs. Or because she was thinking about her commandant father and her commandant mother and Gregory and moon chameleons and the end of the world. Or because of the breathing, snoring and wheezing noises coming from the other bunks around her. It was the other sound. Not the sound of the wind whistling in the hang glider parked on the lawn outside, which Petter had said they could keep before he had rushed off towards downtown Klæbu to drink hot chocolate and play poker. It was another sound, a clicking sound. She couldn't figure out what it was, but it sounded like it was coming from somewhere inside the cabin.

"Nilly," she whispered.

But Nilly's only response was a whistling snoring sound.

Lisa kicked off the covers and snuck over to the door and out into the hallway. She stood there for a while listening, the ice-cold floor hurting the soles of her feet.

The sound was coming from a door that was ajar at the end of the hallway.

She snuck over to the door and peeked in.

The first thing she saw was a jacket hanging over the back of a chair. It was Butler Åke's tailcoat. Someone was sitting in the chair, with his back to Lisa, gently and rhythmically hitting something that looked like a stapler, but which Lisa recognised. It was a Morse code telegraph key. Her commandant father had one just like it at Akershus Fortress. They had used it during the war to transmit messages, kind of like how people send text messages today. Her dad had even taught her the Morse code alphabet. Three short, three long and three short spelled "SOS," for example. And "hi!" was four short and then two short. But who in the world was Butler Åke sending messages to at this time of the night? Lisa froze when she saw Butler Åke's hand. If that was his hand. It had abnormally long fingers that were covered with grey hair and ended in black fingernails.

Lisa's eyes slid down over the back of the chair. And there, through the top of the slit between the tails at the bottom of his tailcoat, she saw something oozing out between the bars in the chair back. Something pink. In bulging clumps. And even though she'd never seen any before, Lisa knew instinctively what they were: hemorrhoids.

Suddenly the clicking came to an abrupt stop. Lisa quickly ducked back from the doorway. She held her breath and listened, her heart pounding in her chest. Butler Åke was a moon chameleon! Had he heard her? Her fear commanded that she run. But her fearlessness said that if she ran now, he was bound to hear her. Her fearlessness won. She waited, urging her heart to please beat a *little* more quietly. The seconds passed. Nothing happened. Then the Morse code started again.

Lisa exhaled and listened. And counted. And spelled.

S-A-B-B-O-T-E-U-R-S   C-A-M-E   T-O   S-E-E T-H-E   K-I-N-G   (STOP)   T-H-E-Y   W-A-N-T   T-O S-A-V-E   T-H-E   F-R-O-G   (STOP)   W-H-A-T S-H-O-U-L-D   I   D-O?   (STOP).

Lisa waited. Then she heard the clicking sounds of the response:

F-I-L-T-H-Y   P-A-N-T-S!   Y-O-D-O-L-F   S-A-Y-S O-F-F   W-I-T-H   T-H-E-I-R   H-E-A-D-S   A-N-D

E-A-T T-H-E-M F-O-R B-R-E-A-K-F-A-S-T (STOP)
G-O-R-A-N.

Eat them for breakfast!

There was no time to lose; they had to get out of here!

Lisa snuck back down the hallway with infinite care. A floorboard creaked. She thought she heard the door behind her slide open, but didn't dare turn around. *Commandant Daddy,* she thought. *Commandant Daddy, SOS, SOS!*

The Vincibles Are Made into Mincemeat. Maybe.

THE KING WAS dreaming that there was a gala dinner at the Royal Palace. There was pomp and glamour and government cabinet members bowing and curtsying, and he was wearing his dress uniform with the diagonal silk band and his chest full of medals. And he had just explained to his dinner companion,

Mrs Strobe, that one of the medals was called the "little seahorse" when he felt something shaking his chair. And when he looked up it was that chiropractor, Tenorsen. The singing one. Hallvard Tenorsen.

"You're in my chair," Tenorsen said. "Move!"

The king stood his ground, but Tenorsen kept shaking and shaking.

"Wake up, Your Royalness!"

The king opened his eyes. And was looking right at Butler Åke's face.

"You have to come, Your Royalness. Your guests have locked themselves in their room. I need the keys."

"Locked themselves in? Why in the world . . ."

"I don't know, but they won't open the door. They're planning something. I think they may have been sent by Tenorsen."

Tenorsen! The king jumped out of bed, pulled on his dressing gown, stuck his hand down into the chamber pot next to his bed, and pulled out a ring of keys.

"Aha," Åke said, reaching for the keys.

"I'm coming too," the king said.

It wasn't until they'd walked down the hall towards the guest room that the king noticed the large, rusty sword Åke was lugging around with him.

"What's that for?" he asked.

"To chop off their heads. In case they resist, I mean."

"That won't be necessary," the king said, knocking on the door. "I'm sure there's been some kind of mis-understanding. Rosemarie! This is Your Royalness! What's going on?"

No response.

The king turned to Åke. "Why did you need to go into their room in the middle of the night anyway?"

"To chop off – uh, to check if their chamber pots needed emptying."

"Oh, right," the king said. He found the right key on his ring, stuck it in the keyhole, and twisted. "Rosemarie! I'm coming in now!"

He pulled down on the door handle and had only just opened the door when Butler Åke rushed past him into the room with his sword raised over his head.

"Don't . . ." the king said, but it was too late. There was a tearing sound as the sword sliced through the fabric on one of the duvets and a cloud of feathers flew into the air. And then another duvet. And then another.

"Butler Åke!" the king yelled.

"Butler King!" Åke mocked in return, laughed loudly and resoundingly, stabbing again and again. "I'm making breakfast, Your Royal Highness," Åke snorted.

The king could hardly see him anymore in the snow-storm of feathers. But he could see the open window next to the bunk beds. Åke had stopped stabbing and roared a furious "Where are they, those human cowards?"

In the silence that followed, the king heard the voice of the red-haired one: "Three, two, one."

Butler Åke stormed over to the window.

"There you are!"

"Zero."

"I'm going to make carpacci—"

There was a boom. The cabin shook.

"Wh-wh-what was that?" the king stammered.

Åke slowly turned to face the king. His face was covered with a layer of white powdery snow. "That," he said, as the snow tumbled out of his mouth, "was the rebels getting away. But you're not going to."

"Your Royal Highness," the king reminded.

"What?" Åke asked, more snow falling off his face.

"You forgot to say Your Royal . . ." The king was staring at Åke's face. It was completely unrecognisable. It was black with grey hair, a prominent chin and an open mouth with sharp, shiny teeth.

"PHEW, THAT WAS a close call," Doctor Proctor said, pulling off his nightcap, putting on his swimming goggles and steering the hang glider around one small, solitary cumulus cloud. "Is everyone here?"

"I'm here," said Mrs Strobe.

"I'm here," Lisa said.

"And I'm here," Nilly said.

Nilly stuck his head out of the sleeping bag and looked down. South Trøndelag was disappearing behind them and below them the moonlight was glittering on snow-covered peaks and iced-over lakes. It had all happened so fast he wasn't truly awake yet. He had just barely managed to pull on his pants and one shoe, the other was in his jacket pocket. Nilly felt for it to make sure. He found his mittens and his scarf. And . . .

"Perry!"

"What was that, Nilly?"

"I forgot Perry! He's still back at the cabin!"

"Whoops," Doctor Proctor said. "It's too late to go

back now. But if I know Perry, I'm sure he managed to hide."

Nilly tore at his hair and wailed, "But what will he do without us?"

"Catch flies and steer clear of that baboon until this is all over," Lisa said. "I promise that we'll go back and get him, Nilly."

"Lisa's right," Doctor Proctor said. "What we need to do now is get back to Oslo. Save Gregory. And the world. And then – if we haven't been eaten for breakfast yet by that point – Perry."

"Poor Perry," Mrs Strobe said. "And poor, poor Nilly."

Nilly pulled his head back into the sleeping bag and moped the whole way, until Lisa yelled, "Look, it's Elverum! We're getting there!" and he stuck his head out again and looked down at the small town they were soaring over. A red stripe had appeared under all the blackness in the east. A new day was dawning. Nilly decided to stop moping. After all, there wasn't anything they could do. You always lose something in war, but life goes on. It must go on. And the scene around them was so beautiful that there was no time to lose for those who loved life.

Hiccups and
Hard Landings

AS THE SUN rose over South Trøndelag, the king lay on his back on the bunk bed, staring at a cobweb on the ceiling. And since he was a king who was dying for some company and who was completely alone, regrettably confined behind locked window shutters and a locked door with no one else to talk to, he figured he might as well talk to the spider who was sitting in the middle of the web.

"A baboon . . . who would've thought? Would you believe my butler is a villainous, talking baboon."

"Hiccup!" the spider said.

"Exactly," the king said. "Maybe I'm crazy, because I just thought I heard a spider hiccup."

"Hiccup!" the spider said.

"Thanks," the king said. "You look pretty alone and forsaken yourself. Did you hear what that baboon said? That he'd been tricking me the whole time, that he was a spy assigned to keep an eye on what I was doing and who came to visit me. Have you ever heard of such a thing?"

"Hiccup-hiccup."

"What do you think that baboon is going to do to us now?"

But apparently the spider didn't have an answer for this question. At least, it didn't hiccup.

"Yeah, yeah," the king said, and stretched. He thought that if you just looked at things the right way there was always a bright side. At least no one could scold him for lounging around in bed, and there was nothing he liked better than lounging around in bed. Well, apart from doing crossword puzzles, of course. And now he wouldn't have to write those speeches either. Boy, he was a lazy king. Not much you could do about that, though. The king closed his eyes, already feeling a little more at ease now that he'd had these thoughts. He tried not to think about the sword Åke had poked under his nose, and about the sound of the key rotating in the keyhole as he had been locked in. The rest of the night he had heard Åke tapping away on that Morse code machine he kept at the end of the hall. *Clack, clack, stop. Clackety clack, stop, clack.* But when he'd tried to peek out through the keyhole to see what was going on, he saw that the key had been left in the hole on the other side of the door and was blocking his view. He sniffed. What was that smell? Waffles? No, not waffles, the smell of grease on a waffle iron that was heating up. Well, well, at least there would be waffles for breakfast.

This thought made the king feel a little better, and he started to fall asleep.

"Ouch!"

His eyes snapped open. The spider was sitting on his nose, staring at him with its eight black eyes.

"D-d-did you just bite me?"

"Hiccup!"

"What do you mean?"

Without hiccuping in response, the spider darted across the duvet, down the bedpost, across the floor, up the door and vanished through the keyhole.

"Strange animal," the king mumbled, closing his eyes. And then he heard it again. The sound of a key twisting around in the keyhole. Breakfast! He waited for the door to open, but nothing happened. Instead, the spider appeared in the keyhole again. It was pulling a glossy strand of cobweb behind it.

"Hiccup!"

"Hiccup this and hiccup that," the king said, rolling over to face the wall. He yawned, closed his eyes and felt a nice dream about chocolate éclairs and cream-filled buns coming on. But was that really the sound of a key turning in the lock? The king opened his eyes again. And what did that have to do with the spider? That strand of cobweb . . . that couldn't be. The king got out of bed and tiptoed over to the door. Cautiously pressed down the handle. And pushed the door . . . open! The door was open! He looked at the key, which was on the outside, and at the cobwebs that had been spun around the end of the key. Had that spider really managed to turn this large key using cobweb?

From the door that was ajar at the end of the hall came the sounds of Morse code. *Clack, clack, stop.* And the king realised that this was his chance, his chance to escape! He pulled on his shoes and tied the laces. But then it occurred to him: Escape from what? From waffles for breakfast? He needed to think about this. He didn't quite see the point in escaping. Still, there was something bugging him about what that redheaded boy had said. About his being king. And he couldn't actually smell any waffle batter, just the waffle iron. He tiptoed over to the front door of the cabin but stopped suddenly. His shoes were making shockingly loud clacking sounds. He listened, but the Morse code from the next room was still going. He concentrated on making his footsteps coincide with the clacking sounds from the Morse code machine. This wasn't easy. *Clack, clack, stop. Clickety clack, stop, clack.* It turned into a bizarre dance, but finally he reached the door. He grabbed his car keys, which were hanging on the key holder on the wall, grabbed his ermine coat, which was hanging from the coat rack, and was about to sneak out when he felt something poke him on the back of the neck. He froze until he realised that it wasn't Åke's sword, it was the spider! It had climbed up onto him and was now seated on his white ermine collar.

"You're hired, buddy," the king whispered. "And Butler Åke is fired."

And with that he trundled off as quickly as he could down the path towards the old black Rolls Royce that had been given to his great-grandfather as a gift from the king of England and the British Empire. He slid in behind the wheel and put the key in the ignition. Suddenly he wished he had one of those reliable little Japanese cars that always started, but they would just have to cross their fingers. He pulled out the choke, pumped the accelerator and twisted the key in the ignition.

The starter complained. *Oink, oink, oink.*

Just then there was a loud cry from the cabin. "Hey! Stop! Your Royalness!"

The king tried again. *Oink, oink, double oink.*

"Into the waffle iron with you! I need my breakfast!"

The king stomped desperately on the accelerator, because in the rearview mirror he saw an enormous and buck naked baboon rapidly approaching.

"Start already, you lousy British lemon!" the king frantically exclaimed.

The baboon filled his rearview mirror as the engine finally started. The king let out the clutch, lurched down the driveway and skidded out onto the main road.

"Phew! That was close, buddy," the king said, looking in his rearview mirror. All he saw was the cabin, no baboon.

"Hiccup!" said the spider, which had climbed up onto the dashboard.

"What is it, buddy?" The king checked his mirror again. And swore quietly and regally. Just barely visible over the trunk he saw two pointy, hairy ears and some gray bangs. That baboon was on his rear bumper.

Didn't that ape know that South Trøndelag traffic rules strictly forbade anyone from riding like that? The king looked ahead again. And he spotted something up there and felt a hopeful smile spread over his face. Then he rolled down his window, floored the gas pedal and screamed at the top of his lungs: "Time for you to hit the road, Åke!"

There was a bang as the speed bump smashed up into the undercarriage of the Rolls Royce, whipping the back end of the car up into the air, kind of like a horse kicking its hind legs. They heard the shriek of a crazed ape, which quickly faded into the distance.

The king looked in his mirror and laughed. He asked the spider, "Hey, buddy, want to see a flying baboon?"

And there – somewhere between South Trøndelag and the sky – a grey baboon hung in the air for a short moment before it started its journey back down.

"Let's get ourselves to Norway," the king said, accelerating.

FOR THE LAST half hour the four Vincibles had pretty much just seen forest below them. A couple of lakes, occasionally a road, but almost no houses. They'd been gradually losing altitude, and now the hang glider was starting to fly dangerously low over the treetops.

"I'm afraid we're not going to make it to Oslo," Doctor Proctor said.

"There's a clearing just ahead!" Nilly shouted.

And sure enough, the blackness of the trees suddenly ended, and below them was a frozen lake. Doctor Proctor steered in for a landing and swung his long legs out of his sleeping bag.

"Tighten your seat belts!" he yelled.

And then they were down. The professor dug his heels into the ice, but the family-size hang glider was so loaded down that he wasn't able to stop it. The vessel tipped over forwards, and a second later they were all lying in a heap on the ice.

"Is everyone okay?" Doctor Proctor yelled, helping Mrs Strobe to her feet.

"One casualty," Nilly said. He was eyeing the hang glider's smashed nose section with distress.

"What are we going to do now?" Lisa asked once she had managed to brush off her clothes and look at the gloomy forest that was hemming them in, surrounding the frozen lake on all sides.

"We'll use the world's best travel invention," Doctor Proctor said.

"What's that?" Nilly asked, excited.

"Legs," Doctor Proctor said, and started walking.

They walked into the woods, wading through the snow until they got in under the trees where the snow wasn't as deep. And kept walking.

After a while they took a breather on a hillside.

"Not that I'm whining or anything," said Mrs Strobe, who had sat down on a stump. "But I lost a shoe in the landing. And I don't know if I can walk much farther."

She hadn't said a word about her sore foot, but now – with the sock pulled down – they saw that it was bloody and swollen.

Just then they heard a familiar noise.

A car.

Then the noise disappeared again.

Nilly ran in the direction the noise had come from and then back again immediately.

"There's a road right up ahead," he said.

They helped Mrs Strobe along and soon reached a narrow gravel road.

"If one car came by, there's bound to be others," Doctor Proctor said.

And so they started waiting. And then they waited some more. Then they continued waiting.

"No one's coming," Lisa sighed after a good deal more waiting.

"Nonsense," Nilly said. "This is exactly like how a watched pot won't boil. You have to stop watching it, then it'll start boiling right away. Come on, let's go back into the woods."

The others hesitantly followed Nilly. And the very moment they reached the edge of the woods, they heard the hum of an engine approaching on the road.

"What did I tell you?" Nilly yelled, racing back to the road.

And, sure enough, there was a car coming.

"We'll hitchhike, then," Doctor Proctor said, sticking out his thumb.

"Well, there's hitchhiking and then there's hitch-hiking," Nilly said, positioning himself in the middle of the narrow road and waving both his arms.

And ten seconds later, they were sitting in a warm car.

"This was so nice of you," Mrs Strobe said, and then sneezed.

"No trouble at all," the driver said. "So what takes you to Oslo?"

"We're going to rescue Gregory Galvanius," Nilly said. "And Norway. And the rest of the world, for that matter. How about you?"

"Me? I got a letter from the army telling me to report to the Royal Palace. They're going to give us uniforms and rifles and send us to Denmark."

"Are you sure that's a . . . good idea?" Lisa asked from where she sat squeezed into the backseat.

The driver looked at her in the mirror. "It's a great idea. If vee don't conquer them, they'll come conquer us. Haven't you been listening to the president?"

"Ah, now that you mention that," Doctor Proctor said, "would it be all right if we turned on the radio?"

"Of course," the man said, flipping on the radio. Choral singing poured from the speakers. Doctor Proctor turned to the next radio station. Choral singing. And to the next. More choral singing. Doctor Proctor kept flipping through, but it didn't do any good. There was choral singing on every station.

"Whish station did you want to listen to?" the driver asked.

"We want to hear the king's speech," Doctor Proctor said.

The driver gave the professor a weird look. "What king?"

"The king."

"I don't know about any king."

The other passengers in the car froze.

Doctor Proctor cleared his throat. "I'm sure you would recognise the king's voice if you heard it. And understand that what he says about not listening to Hallvard Tenorsen is sensible."

The professor practically slammed his forehead against the windshield as the driver slammed on the brakes. They had pulled to a sudden stop in the middle of the road.

"I think this is where you get out," the driver said, leaning over Doctor Proctor to open the door.

"But . . ."

"Out! I won't have traitors in my car."

"WELL, WELL," SIGHED Doctor Proctor as he and the other three Vincibles watched the car disappear in the heavy snowfall. Then they started trudging down the road. But around each bend they just saw more trees, more snow, more bends.

They walked. And shivered. And walked. And shivered. They tried walking away from the road into the woods a couple of times, but no cars came. So they walked more. And shivered more.

"Won't there be a bus soon?" Lisa sighed.

"Won't there be breakfast soon?" Nilly asked, spitting out the pine needles he'd been chewing on.

"W-w-w-" – the teeth in Mrs Strobe's mouth chattered – "won't it be summer soon?"

And then – at long last – they finally heard a noise. Then a little more noise. Then really a lot of noise.

"Wh-wh-what could that be?" Mrs Strobe asked, and then sneezed.

"Hm," Doctor Proctor said and looked up at the sky. "A squadron of bombers might sound like that. Maybe they're already on their way to Denmark."

Lisa moaned in despair: "Oh no! We're not going to manage to save anything at all."

The noise came closer and closer.

"Get out of the open!" Doctor Proctor said. "Into the trees!"

"Wait," Nilly said. "That's not bombers. It's an A major. A *perfect* A major, in fact."

They stopped and stared back at the last bend in the road.

And then it came into view. A roaring motorcycle with the biggest sidecar anyone has ever seen. A whole theatre box with room to seat a whole little orchestra, actually.

And sitting behind the wheel was a man they

recognised. Despite the outdated red jacket with the white fur collar he was wearing.

"Y-y-your Royal Highness!" Mrs Strobe cried out, her teeth chattering.

Even from quite a distance they could see the man behind the steering wheel light up and start braking. The motorcycle slid sideways, then a little backwards, then kind of sideways, and then definitely forwards, before it finally came to a stop right in front of them.

"Perry!" Nilly cried when he spotted his seven-legged friend on the man's white collar.

"Rosemarie!" the king cried. "And . . . and . . ." However, it was clear that he didn't remember the name of a single one of the others, so he gave up: "And all you others! You have no idea what happened after you left. I . . ."

"Wait," Doctor Proctor said. "There's not much time. Tell us the story while we're driving. Everyone into the sidecar!" The professor looked down at the king and added, "And *I'll* drive."

"But . . . but I'm the king!"

"It's my motorcycle," Doctor Proctor said, swinging his leg over the bike in front of the king and using his rear end to nudge the king farther back on the seat. "Everyone in?"

And as a unanimous "yes!" rose from the sidecar, Doctor Proctor revved the engine and they sped off.

Plan B for Nilly

AND AS THEY drove, the king told his story as loudly as he could so that they could hear him over the engine.

About his escape in the Rolls Royce. And how the crossing arm had been down when he got to the border, and two strange border guards had said that no one could come in, especially not kings. And how the king had turned around and on his way back had picked up a hitchhiker in red leotards.

"He shouted that his name was Petter, and that he'd lost all his money playing poker in Klæbu, and that he longed to go back home to his house and all his hang gliders."

So the king had driven Petter home, and after Petter had served the king some hot chocolate and beat him at Chinese checkers four times (each time shouting "I'm the one and only Petter and a heck of a Petter I am!"), he'd rowed the king across the river and told him to follow the high-voltage lines and he'd make it into Norway unseen. So the king had followed some footprints in the snow, and they'd led to a red house where an old man lived who said he was a border smuggler and also a healer who cured people by the laying on of hands.

"And he was the one who sold me this motorcycle," the king said.

"Sold?" Doctor Proctor exclaimed. "He sold you *my* motorcycle?"

"Yup. For one thousand one hundred and eleven krone. Plus the laying on of hands. He cured me of arthritis of the liver and rectal bronchitis, actually. Clever chap. I wasn't even aware I had them!"

They zoomed through the forest, and after a couple of intersections, they emerged onto a slightly wider road with fewer trees. Little by little they started seeing a few more cars. And then a few more. And then finally they saw a sign that read:

OSLO 7 MILES

WHEN THE CLOCK on the tower on Oslo City Hall struck three, the motorcycle was parked outside Syvertsen's Pastries. And after the woman whose name wasn't Marete poured them more tea and Mrs Strobe's teeth had stopped chattering and Nilly had eaten two and a half breakfasts, Doctor Proctor cleared his throat and said:

"So, what we know is that if we're going to rescue Gregory, the country, and the world for that matter, we have to act fast. Unfortunately, what we don't know is where Gregory is or what Yodolf's plans for attacking Denmark are. And without that information, it may be hard for us to save anyone or anything at all."

"Too bad you don't know Morse code," Lisa told the king. "Then you could've told us what Butler Åke was saying."

"All I remember was that I was trying to sneak out of the cabin in time to the clicking from the device," the king sighed, his mouth full of waffle. "It was like 'clickety' and 'click-click-click-click' something-or-other."

"Well, that would be a *T* and then an *H*," Lisa said. "But that's not much help."

"You know Morse code?" the king asked, clearly impressed.

Lisa nodded. "Don't you remember even the tiniest bit more?"

"Let me rack my brains," the king said, and started making faces.

"Hiccup-hiccup-hiccup hic-hic-hic!"

"That's an *O* and an *S*," Lisa said.

"I didn't say anything," the king protested, giving up on his brain racking with a moan.

"Hic. Hiccup-hic hic-hic hiccup-hic hiccup-hic-hiccup-hic hiccup-hiccup-hiccup hiccup-hiccup."

Five pairs of pupils were all trained on Nilly. And Nilly's two pupils were directed upwards, trying to see the top of his own head, where Perry was sitting, hiccuping away:

"Hic-hiccup-hiccup-hic hiccup-hiccup-hiccup hiccup-hiccup-hiccup hic-hiccup-hiccup-hic hic-hic-hic."

"*E*," Lisa said. "And NINCOMPOOPS."

"THOSE NINCOMPOOPS!" Nilly shouted eagerly.

"Perry remembers the Morse code! Do you have any more, Perry?"

And Perry did have more. Eventually Lisa had to get out a pen to keep the letters straight. And when Perry finally finished, she read what she'd written on her napkin:

"Those nincompoops are coming to Oslo to rescue that crazy frog."

Mrs Strobe blew her nose into a big handkerchief. "Wescue dat cwazy fwog?" she sputtered, severely congested and raising her hand in the air for clarification.

"There's more," Lisa said. "This is obviously the response from Oslo: *The nincompoops will be too late, ha ha. Because we've got him locked up in the palace's tower dungeon and we will be cooking him for breakfast first thing tomorrow. We're playing BABA music to keep him subdued. Looking forwards to a nice waffle breakfast before we invade Denmark. Keep an eye on the King Dope."*

"King Dope?!" scoffed the king, raising his hand as well.

"We have to save Mr Galvanius before they turn him into waffles," Nilly said.

"They figured out that listening to BABA music saps his strength," Lisa said.

"Poow, poow, poow dawing, dawing, sweet Gwegowy," said Mrs Strobe, drying a tear from her eye. The king looked at her in astonishment.

"Your Royal Highness," Doctor Proctor said. "You have to give a speech on TV. Now, right away! You have to use all your royal influence to get people to storm the Royal Palace before the waffles are made in the morning!"

"Oh yeah?" asked the king, who was still staring at the sobbing Mrs Strobe. His face had also taken on a greenish tint. "To save that poor, poor, darling, darling, SWEET man? As if a king doesn't have more important things to do?"

"Oh, but Youw Woyal Highness," sniffled Mrs Strobe, taking the napkin that Lisa had been writing on. "You *have* to."

"I *do*, Rosemarie?" the king asked, crossing his arms. "And what if I don't?"

Rosemarie looked at the king for a long time. Then she inhaled. She sort of puffed herself up before putting the napkin under her long nose and releasing the air in a long elephant-trumpet of a blow that caused her nostrils to vibrate, the chandeliers to clink and everyone in Syvertsen's Pastries to look around their tables in fear. Then she aimed her Strobe Stare at the king.

But the king shook his head decisively: "Just go right ahead with the brain boiling. I'm not saving any nincompoop of a man I don't even know, but who you're obviously so head over heels in love with that you're willing to do anything for."

Mrs Strobe gaped and completely lost the Strobe Stare. "You think . . . you think that I'm in love with . . ."

"It's obvious to all of us," the king said. "And it wounds me, Rosemarie." His voice was suddenly on the verge of tears. "It wounds me *profoundly*, I'll have you know. I mean, I'm the king, aren't I? And what's he? A frog? I'm sorry, Rosemarie, but this is awfully humiliating. You'll have to clean this mess up yourself."

Mrs Strobe and the others stared dumbfounded at the king, who stood up, brushed the cake crumbs off his jacket, marched out and slammed the door shut behind him so the little bell on it jerked and tinkled.

"Well, that didn't go very well, did it?" Doctor Proctor said.

"What do we do now?" Lisa sighed.

"Simple," said Nilly and leaped up onto the table. "Now the Vincibles implement Plan B of course."

"Which is?"

"Well, there's *is* and then there's *is*," Nilly said. "Naturally we have to come up with the plan first.

But it'll be stupendous. Nilly's Plan B. A delightful, small, freckly plan. Just as ingenious as it is elegant and simple. To put it briefly: a Plan B that is so good no one will believe it wasn't our Plan A!"

Doctor Proctor cleared his throat. "If you're done advertising your plan, maybe we could get started coming up with it."

"Of course," Nilly said, hopping back down off the table. "Anyone have any ideas?"

It was quiet around the table for a long time.

Finally Mrs Strobe began: "What if we go up the dungeon towew, unlock the doow and . . . uh, welease Gwegowy?"

"Well, that is certainly simple, Mrs Strobe," Nilly said. "But – with all due respect – maybe not that ingenious or elegant. Unless you have a strong desire to see yourself made into waffles, that is. That tower is more closely guarded than the Bank of Norway, and besides they know we're on our way to rescue

Gregory. We have to outwit them somehow. Any other suggestions?"

It was quiet for so long that they could hear the second hand on the clock on the wall. The second hand was ticking towards what they knew was going to happen if they didn't come up with something ingenious and outwitful.

"I think maybe I have something," Lisa said.

"What?" everyone else asked in unison.

"Let's go to a hotel," Lisa said.

The Hotel and the Great Escape Attempt

IT WAS NIGHTTIME in Oslo, and the moon hung in a cloudless but star-packed sky like a yellowish-white paper lantern. It shone on the twenty-story-high Radisson Hotel next to Palace Park, on the not-quite-so-high dungeon tower at the Royal Palace, and also on the large, shiny device that sat just inside the gate, a device that bore an uncanny and frightening similarity to a waffle iron, only a hundred times bigger. And the moon shone on the gateway leading into the Royal Palace's rear courtyard, which was guarded by two mustache-wearing men in black Royal Guard uniforms with lame hats with big, floppy tassels.

"Truly beautiful sky vee have here in Norway," said the one with the handlebar mustache. "Don't you agree, Gunnar?"

"I would have to say that I agree, Rolf," the one with the Fu Manchu mustache said. "No one has stars as beautiful as ours in Norway."

"Yes, just knowing that God shose to bless our specific country with sush a beautiful sky truly moves me, you know?"

"Not surprising, really, that the Danes want to take a sky like that from us."

"From us, the Birthplace of Shampions, it's an insult! I must say I'm looking forward to oblisterating them."

"I think that's supposed to be 'obliterating,' Rolf."

"Yes, you're quite right, Gunnar. And then, of course, I'm looking forward to the execution first thing tomorrow morning."

"I wonder what that froggy fellow is thinking right about now," said Gunnar with the Fu Manchu.

They both cast a quick glance up at the dungeon tower, which was silhouetted against the starry sky.

"Strange," Fu Manchu said, stamping his feet. "For a second I thought I saw a little boy hanging in the sky up there."

"Ho ho ho," Handlebar said.

NILLY STOOD STOCK-STILL and kept his balance. He had stopped suddenly when those two guards down below had looked up. Had they seen him? Hopefully not.

He felt a slight vibration in the taut, almost invisible cobweb beneath the balancing shoes. He carefully turned the other way, to face the Radisson Hotel. More specifically room 1146, where the strand of cobweb disappeared into the window and was anchored around the minibar in the corner. And in the darkness, he could just make out the silhouettes of Lisa, Doctor Proctor and Mrs Strobe in the window. Then he turned back around to face forwards again, towards the dungeon tower. There was always a lot more wind up at these heights than you would guess if you were standing on solid ground. But tonight the wind had helped him.

It had been twenty minutes since all five of them had rushed into the hotel and asked for a room high up with a view of the Royal Palace. And luckily room 1146 had been available. So the front desk clerk gave them a key card, and they took the elevator up to the eleventh floor. From there they implemented Lisa's plan. Lisa had read somewhere that when spiders wanted to cover long distances, they would just spin themselves a cobweb sail and use that to fly on the wind. And Mrs Strobe had nodded and said that that was actually true. And that was precisely what Perry had done. While Doctor Proctor checked that the wind was blowing in more or less the right direction, the enterprising, clever spider had spun his own little hang glider, anchored it to the minibar and jumped out the window. And instead of plummeting down into a puddle of spider jam on the pavement eleven stories below them, Perry had sailed off towards the Palace Park and disappeared into the nighttime darkness with a little hiccup.

They had waited for almost ten minutes before they finally got the signal: three tugs on the thread, meaning that Perry had made it to the dungeon tower at the Royal Palace and secured the thread.

Then it was Nilly's turn. Because of course it would be Nilly's job to go over, who else? This time the others gave up as soon as he pointed out that he was the only one of them they *knew* was light enough for Perry's cobweb to hold and that maybe he would even be small enough to squeeze through the bars into Gregory's cell.

So Nilly strapped on the balancing shoes and cautiously stepped out onto the delicate strand of cobweb.

"Here," Doctor Proctor had said, passing him the pink Double Deaf Earmuffs and a small bottle labelled "Doctor Proctor's Strength Tonic with Mexican Thunder Chili. Maximum Strength."

And then Nilly started walking. And kept walking until he saw the two guards at the gate suddenly look up. And then he stopped. And thus we're back where we were, with Nilly standing stock-still on the thread and the guard with the handlebar mustache laughing at the guard with the Fu Manchu mustache because for a second Fu Manchu had thought he'd seen a little boy up there in midair.

Nilly exhaled with relief when he realised that he hadn't been detected after all, and then he continued his balancing act, making his way over to the dungeon tower.

He heard music. And a familiar woman's voice singing:

> *"Pizzeria, have a slice to go*
> *Extra cheese, how can I refuse it . . ."*

And there – in the darkness, through a narrow slit – he saw Perry's eight black eyes twinkling.

Nilly crept the last bit of the way, hopped up onto the balcony that ran around the top of the tower, and waited for Perry to crawl up on top of his hair before squeezing his head through the bars into the window opening.

It was a dark cell with bare stone walls. But there – in the gleaming moonlight and the flickering light of a candle – he saw Gregory Galvanius. He was tied up on the wall with iron shackles around his wrists and ankles. Aside from a pair of long johns that was white – or at least pretty white – he was naked. His skinny upper body was the same bluish-white colour as milk, and his already sad face looked even sadder with the blondish-brown stubble and the blue-black bags under his eyes.

"Mr Galvanius," Nilly whispered.

No response.

"Gregory! We're here to rescue you."

Poor Gregory lifted his face extremely slowly and stared at Nilly blankly at first. Then – as if it slowly dawned on him that this really was Nilly and not just a dream – his face lit up.

Nilly squeezed through the bars and – *shloop* – he was in.

"Lookie here," he said, holding up the pink earmuffs. "We'll put these on you and then you won't hear the music. And then you take a swig of this . . ." He screwed the top off the bottle of strength tonic. "Maximum strength. Enough that you'll be able to break open both the iron shackles and the door out of here. But we have to hurry; the others are waiting."

He was about to put the earmuffs on Gregory when he noticed a sudden change in Gregory's expression.

Or more like a transformation. Because there, before Nilly's very eyes, Gregory Galvanius's face suddenly got smaller. And rounder. And then the stubble and the bags under his eyes disappeared and the face was suddenly freckled, with a turned-up nose. And finally: hair so red it could only belong to one single boy Nilly knew of.

Himself.

Nilly stood there staring at his own mirror image. And then his mirror image started laughing. It opened its mouth, sharp teeth came into view, and a pink tongue flapped around in there as laughter forced its way out, drowning out Agnes's singing. And when Nilly looked down, he spotted two pairs of holey socks with curved black toenails poking through them. And a long, grey-haired tail swishing back and forth just above the stone floor.

"Aaaaah!" Nilly screamed.

"Hiccup!" Perry said.

"Double aaaaah!" Nilly screamed.

"Hiccup hiccup!" they heard from somewhere else.

The chortling, betailed mirror image of Nilly stepped aside and there he hung, the real Gregory. His eyes were half closed, as if he had half fainted.

"I've been waiting and longing for this visit," Nilly's mirror image said, and Nilly recognised the voice from the Royal Palace. It was the boss himself: Yodolf Staler. And then the face and body of the creature changed. And turned into Hallvard Tenorsen, who then assumed an apologetic expression: "But I'm also a little sad, because our acquaintance is going to be so short-lived. Unfortunately, you're both going to be made into waffles tomorrow."

Just then the door opened, and in bounded four moon baboons. It happened so fast that Nilly wouldn't even have had a chance to say "cake," if he'd felt like doing that. Well, that's an exaggeration; he *would* have been able to say "cake." But maybe not "layer cake." Or certainly not "frosted layer cake." Because before he

would have had a chance to say "frosted layer cake" —
if he *had* wanted to say that — the baboons had picked
Nilly up and shackled him to the wall next to Gregory.
So now they were dangling there like wallflowers, the
two of them.

Yodolf walked over to Nilly, cocked his head and
peered at him as if he were wondering what kind of
strange creature this could be. Then he plucked Perry
out of Nilly's hair, held the spider between his thumb
and index finger and looked like he was considering
crushing the seven-legged thingamajig. But he changed
his mind and instead dumped the strength tonic out
of Doctor Proctor's bottle, put the spider into the
bottle, screwed the lid back on and set the bottle on
the window ledge.

"Now you can watch as your friend slowly suffocates
in there," Yodolf said.

Then he stretched his hand out through the bars,
grabbed hold of the cobweb thread and pulled it

towards him. "Hm," he said thoughtfully. "Tandoora, can you run out and see where this cobweb originates? If my guess is right, I bet the rest of the accomplices will be at the other end."

"I'll run and check right away, Yodolf," the smallest moon baboon said, and then disappeared, shuffling quickly away.

Yodolf bit through the strand of cobweb with an obvious "snap!" and let it fall out the window. Then he put on the pink earmuffs and listened to the silence, but apparently decided that silence is boring, because he took them off again and tossed them over to one of the other baboons, who tried them on. Yodolf stretched in satisfaction, his arms thrust into the air, and yawned, revealing jaws so large that they could have easily accommodated a watermelon.

"Time for bed. We have a long day ahead of us tomorrow," Yodolf said. "No wait, ha ha! I forgot. You're actually going to have a very short day."

"Good one!" yelled one of the baboons in a squeaky voice Nilly recognised. Then all three baboons howled with laugher.

"You stand guard, Göran," Yodolf said.

"Me? But I'm the . . ."

"Commander of the Luftwaffle, I know. But I'm still the one who makes the decisions, right? Hop to it, now! We're going to go see what Tandoora found."

And with that Yodolf chased the other moon baboons out the door ahead of him, locked the door and passed the key ring to Göran.

"Would it be all right if I just . . ." Göran began.

"No," Yodolf growled. "You may *not* torture them. They taste better untortured."

Göran muttered a scarcely audible "filthy britches" and snatched the key ring, and then the other baboons were gone. Nilly heard the scraping of chair legs as Göran sat down somewhere out in the hallway and turned up the music.

"Yeah, yeah," Nilly said. "Sometimes that's just how it goes."

"I think that's how it goes *every* time, if you ask me," Gregory sniffed. "Oh, if only they'd turn off that music!"

"I'm sure the others will be along soon to rescue us," Nilly tried, but Gregory interrupted him in irritation: "Have you seen the guards around the Palace, huh? They have fifty moon chameleons and a hundred hypnotised Norwegians with rifles running around in traditional waterproof Norwegian boots. Forget about it! We're toast!"

Nilly sighed heavily and bit his tongue since it was obvious that Gregory was not in a chatty mood. After a while he heard the guard out there in the hallway start snoring.

"Hey!" Nilly whispered. "I have an idea!"

"Oh no," Gregory groaned. "I can't take any more."

"It's simple," Nilly said. "All you have to do is just unfurl your tongue."

26

Banister and Camel Poop

"OH NO," LISA said. "They're prisoners!"

Doctor Proctor and Mrs Strobe, who were standing next to Lisa, were staring out into the darkness from the window of room 1146 at the Radisson Hotel. Doctor Proctor's hand was still clutching the loose cobweb they'd pulled back in, once they'd realised that the other end had been bitten off.

"And soon we may be prisoners, too," Doctor Proctor said. "Yodolf has most certainly figured out that this web leads here. We have to get out of here. And how!"

And with that he let go of the strand of cobweb and ran out of room 1146 with the others fast on his heels. They stopped at the end of the hallway to wait for the elevator.

"We'w in luck!" Mrs Strobe said, and pointed to the illuminated numbers over the lift door. "De elevatow is on its way ub."

"What if it's full of moon chameleons on their way up?" Lisa said.

"Nonsense, dey're not dat fast," Mrs Strobe said.

It was quiet. The display showed that the lift was moving from the seventh to the eighth floor.

"On the other hand," Doctor Proctor said. "It is healthier to take the stairs."

The lift was on the ninth floor.

"Stair climbing is very good for you," Lisa said.

Tenth floor.

"Taking de staiws will help you liw longew," Mrs Strobe said.

"Come on," Doctor Proctor urged.

And they all ran for the door with the green glowing EXIT sign over it and darted out.

The door clicked shut behind them just as they heard a loud, obvious *pling* sound from the lift as its doors slid open.

"The banister," Lisa said, looking down the stairwell where the banister descended in circles, appearing smaller and smaller, until it finally came to an end way down below them on the ground floor. "Nilly would take the banister if he were here."

Then she swung her leg over to sit astride the banister, let go and started careening backwards. And before she'd even reached the first turn, she saw Doctor

Proctor helping Mrs Strobe up onto the banister.

They went around and around, faster and faster. Walls, stairs and fire escape doors swirled past. And Lisa was so dizzy after she plopped onto the floor at the bottom, on the ground floor, that after she managed to stand up she just stood there swaying back and forth. Then Mrs Strobe arrived. *Plop!*

"What happened to Doctor Proctor?" Lisa asked, peering up the stairwell.

And then he appeared. Sliding slowly, squeezing the banister tightly between his thighs as he moaned in pain.

"Don't squeeze so hawd!" Mrs Strobe yelled.

And the professor must have done what she said. Because suddenly he came swishing down and – *plop!* – there he lay too, as the scent of burned trouser fabric spread through the air and he frantically attempted to blow on his thighs.

Lisa heard a door way above them slam and peered up

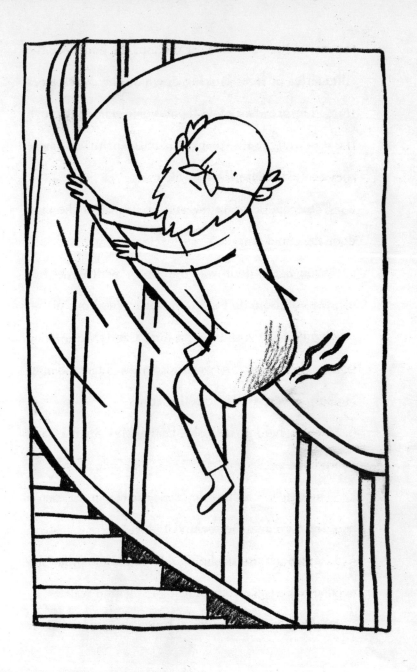

the stairwell. And there, at the top, she could see the silhouettes of faces looking down at her. Black faces framed by grey hair. And then a voice echoed through the stairwell, a voice that said: "Filthy britches! There they are! Back into the lift, hurry!"

"Come on," Lisa urged, running towards the only door she could see.

Through the door was the lobby, which was full of people. Lisa didn't stop, but proceeded out of the revolving door with the professor and Mrs Strobe tight on her heels. They ran across the intersection at Holberg Square to the streetcar stop.

"Dey're behind us!" she heard Mrs Strobe gasp behind her.

"And they're catching up," she heard Doctor Proctor pant from even farther behind.

Lisa ran as fast as she could. She knew what she needed to do to keep from being made into waffles.

So she jumped up, sailed through the air, landed on

the seat of the MWS – Motorcycle With Sidecar – flipped the ignition to ON and stamped as hard as she could on the starter while twisting the accelerator. It didn't start.

She stamped again.

Nothing.

One more time.

Nada.

She heard Mrs Strobe tumble into the sidecar. And saw Doctor Proctor. She looked behind her. She didn't see anyone. But she heard them, heard the rapid shuffling footsteps made by feet with long, unbelievably ugly toenails dragging across the asphalt. The camouflaged beasts were invisible, but obviously hard on their tail.

Lisa jumped up and landed on the starter.

Vrooom!

She'd started it, but what now? Lisa had never driven a motorcycle before.

"Clutch and gear!" Doctor Proctor called out. "Clutch and gear!"

Clutch this, clutch that, Lisa thought, fumbling around on the handles.

The footsteps had reached them. Lisa pressed and shoved. She felt something sit down on the seat behind her and put its arms over her shoulders.

"Like this." It was Doctor Proctor.

The motorcycle surged off the edge of the pavement and down the street.

"MOVE YOUR TONGUE to the right now," whispered Nilly, who had turned his head so that he could see Gregory's bluish frog tongue, which he'd unrolled, through the bars of the cell.

"Whith way?" Gregory groaned with his mouth open.

"To the right. You have to get your tongue around the corner. Göran is sitting a ways down the hallway over there."

"Thith ithn't that eathy," Gregory groaned.

"But you have to do it," Nilly said. "It's our only chance."

Gregory groaned weakly. But managed to roll out more tongue. He also actually managed to get it to turn the corner, where it disappeared from their field of vision.

"And now feel your way forwards," Nilly whispered. "The key ring is probably in his lap."

"Ow!"

"Whath ith it? I mean, what is it?" Nilly asked.

"My tongue ith frothen to the barth."

"Heh?" Nilly said.

"Ow! Ow!" Gregory wailed.

"Shh! You'll wake up Göran," Nilly urged. But at that moment he saw Gregory's tongue and understood what Gregory was trying to tell him. His tongue was stuck to one of the frozen iron bars! He shuddered, thinking back on all the times kids had dared him to touch frozen metal signposts with his tongue. And he'd done it and his tongue was stuck. And he'd got it off again in the most painful way he could imagine. Tearing his tongue free. And that had just been a teeny tiny tongue, whereas Gregory's tongue was . . .

"Yank it free," Nilly urged.

"It hurths," Gregory moaned, on the verge of tears.

"Now!" Nilly said in a stern voice with his eyes closed. And he heard the ripping sound of the surface being torn off Gregory's tongue and saw Gregory's body shudder as he hung there shackled to the cell wall.

"Ow! Ow ow!"

Triple ow! Nilly thought, opening his eyes again. Gregory's frog tongue lay like a piece of blue, frozen whale meat on the cold, dirty stone floor.

"Heroically done, Gregory. Fight on!"

The piece of blue meat wriggled and moved. But then stopped again.

Gregory sighed. "I'm tho tired, Nilly."

"Remember, we're saving the world here, Gregory."

"But I hate thith world!" Gregory wailed.

"So remember you're saving Mrs Strobe here."

Gregory didn't say anything for a minute, then his tongue started moving again.

"I feel a leg. Shinth," Gregory whispered.

"Higher," Nilly said.

"Kneeth," Gregory said.

"Higher."

"Thighth."

"Higher."

"And that'th a . . . a . . . what ith that? Thomething thmooth and bulbouth . . ."

"Uh . . ." said Nilly, who was picturing where Gregory's tongue was at that moment, realising that it was good that Gregory *couldn't* see this for himself. But it was obviously too late.

"Eeeeew!!" Gregory squeezed his eyes shut and spit and spit again.

A steady snoring sound could be heard from out

in the hallway, occasionally combined with a satisfied grunt. And Nilly just couldn't hold it in any longer. He had to laugh. So there hung Nilly, doomed to death, bolted firmly to the wall, shaking with laughter. "Don't give up, Gregory," Nilly whispered, choking with laughter. "Did you find the keys?"

"Thewe!" Gregory said. "I hawe the key wing. It'th in hith lap."

"Good! Bring 'em here."

Nilly watched Gregory's tongue move, slowly rolling up like a streamer, until just the tip of the tongue was sticking out between Gregory's lips. And, sure enough, a key ring was dangling from the tip of the tongue. With keys for anything they might like to unlock, Nilly thought. The padlocks keeping their shackles shut, the barred door to the cell, the main door to the dungeon tower, the back door they could escape through unnoticed. Anything with a lock. There was just one problem.

"How awe we going to unlock the padlockth when we can't even uthe our handth?"

Handth? What was that? Oh, hands! They couldn't use their hands. Nilly hadn't thought that far ahead.

He stared longingly at Perry, who was just looking weaker and weaker, trapped in that bottle. He couldn't help them either.

Freedom was so close and yet so far.

"Freedom is so close," said a voice right by his ear. "And yet so far."

And even though Nilly had been freezing cold for a long time now, the voice made him feel even colder. Yodolf had let himself into the cell so quietly that they hadn't heard him. And they hadn't seen him either. But now portions of the stone wall in front of them changed, and the large baboon-like moon chameleon materialised.

"Now you're going to tell me who your accomplices are," Yodolf said. "And where they're holed up."

Even in this desperate situation, Nilly felt a little shiver of joy. Because Yodolf's question meant that Lisa, Doctor Proctor and Mrs Strobe must have got away!

"Listen here, you clumpy-bummed, unshaven baboon," Nilly said. "You can do whatever you want to me, because I'll never say a word. You're going to make waffles out of us anyway. What could you do that's worse than that?"

"A little torture?" Yodolf said.

"Torture away," Nilly said with a big smile. "Red-heads love pain. Didn't you know that?"

"Hmfrh," Yodolf said, and turned to look at Gregory. "How about you, froggy? Are you a fan of torture? Or what do you say we turn up the volume on the music?"

Nilly eyed Gregory nervously.

"The only thing I want to awoid," Gregory said, the key ring still dangling from the tip of his tongue, "ith mowe baboon hemowhoids. They tathte like camel poop. Othew than that, bwing on the towtuwe."

And Nilly couldn't help it. He had to start laughing again.

Yodolf stared at him in disbelief, slowly shook his head and scoffed, "Humans! You people really aren't normal."

Then he walked over to the window ledge, grabbed the bottle and shook it, jerking a lifeless Perry back and forth.

"Well, in any case, this one is ready," Yodolf said, and chucked the bottle out the window. Nilly held his breath. They heard the bottle break on the cobblestones in the courtyard below. Yodolf pressed his baboon face right up against Nilly's face. "What's wrong, you dwarf? Aren't you laughing anymore?"

Nilly gulped.

Yodolf laughed, snatched the key ring from Gregory's tongue, marched out of the door and slammed it shut and locked behind him.

The King Is King

IT WAS APPROACHING midnight in Oslo. And yet the city hadn't even begun to settle down for the night. As the king strolled towards the palace, he saw people scurrying home with their arms full of food containers, and soldiers driving by in camouflage-coloured trucks. They looked very warlike sitting there in the back of the trucks, staring straight ahead. War-like and kind of hypnotised. And the strange thing was that no one seemed to recognise him even though he was the king. He had just had a small glass of beer at an inn to drown his sorrows about his loved – but alas, lost – Rosemarie. But the waiter had demanded payment even though the king had told the man, "Good Lord, man, I'm the king!" Yes. And it wasn't even just that. He was a king with *a broken heart*! And when the waiter realised that the king only had Swedish money, the man had thrown him out! The king's own subjects didn't recognise him. And he didn't recognise them. It was sad. And when you got right down to it, quite eerie. And now he had to find somewhere to spend the night. He had called a few people he thought were his friends to ask if he could crash with them, but they had all just hung up when they realised who was on the phone. Maybe he should try the Salvation Army. They had a homeless shelter, didn't they?

He walked past a cluster of white stone buildings in the middle of a field. He knew all the buildings so well. The TV and radio headquarters of the Norwegian Broadcasting Corporation. That's where the folks came from who recorded his annual New Year's speech from the Royal Palace. And as if his legs had a will of their own, they proceeded to take him over to those white buildings. In through the revolving door towards the TV studios. And right up to the reception desk.

"I'd like to talk to Nømsk Ull," the king told the female security guard seated behind the counter. She scrutinised him with her strict security guard eyes.

"I don't believe you know him. Nømsk Ull is a big TV star."

"And I'm the king," the king said.

The security guard peered over her glasses and smiled wryly: "Oh you are, huh, sweetie? What did you do, borrow that ermine cape from the costume department?"

The king focused his eyes on her. Not a penetrating Strobe Stare, but a gentle, sleepy look with heavy eyelids. And then he started talking. His words came out in a monotone, sort of a chant, slowly like viscous syrup on a super-cold day:

"My fellow countrymen. The old year is now over and it brought us a great deal, both in terms of progress and reasons to celebrate. For example, our average weight is rising steadily, and Norway is one of the world's happiest countries. We won a gold medal in classic combined Nordic skiing biathlon snow camping, and Honningsvåg has once again been named one of the world's most northerly towns."

The security guard yawned. And the king continued:

"But the year also brought new challenges and problems that we will have to tackle together as a people in the year to come . . ."

The security guard's head nodded forwards a little,

but the king bent over so he could maintain eye contact.

"And right now, there is the issue of saving Norway and the world from catastrophe. Repeat after me: catastrophe."

"Catastrophe," the security guard repeated in a sleep-walker-like voice.

"Which is why," the king said, "you must call Nømsk Ull right now and ask him to come down here."

"Call Nømsk Ull," the security guard repeated. She picked up her phone, dialled a number, waited a moment and then said in that sleepwalking voice, "Please come down to the reception desk."

One minute later, Nømsk Ull, the host of the NoroVision Choral Throwdown, was standing before them.

"I'm always delighted to meet a fan," he crooned with that cheesy grin that was so familiar from the programme, and gave the king an ultra-brief handshake. "But I have to run. Vee're doing a live show right now, and . . ."

He stopped because the king wouldn't let go of his hand.

"Hey, let go. People are waiting and . . ."

"My dear countrymen," the king said, and Nømsk Ull looked at him in surprise. "A new year stands ahead of us and suddenly we find that it is time to express our gratitude for the old one . . ."

Nømsk Ull's eyelids suddenly looked like they had little weights attached to them.

"In the live broadcast you're hosting right now, you will introduce the king, and then the king will address the people of Norway," the king said.

"The king will address the people of Norway," Nømsk Ull repeated.

"Great, let's go do it," the king said.

LISA, DOCTOR PROCTOR and Mrs Strobe sat around the kitchen table in the little blue house, which was surrounded by snowdrifts at the top of Cannon Avenue.

"Phew, that suwe was cloath," Mrs Strobe snuffled, her voice quivering.

"I'm sure glad you handled the clutch and the gears," Lisa told Doctor Proctor.

"It certainly is unfortunate that Nilly and Perry are probably going to be made into waffles along with Gregory tomorrow," Doctor Proctor replied, running both hands through his unruly, bushy hair and scratching his scalp in despair.

"It's mostly my fault," Lisa said. "It was my plan."

"I should've stopped it," Mrs Strobe said. "So I suppose actually it was my . . ."

"Enough!" Doctor Proctor yelled, and then groaned: "Why does one of us always end up in a dungeon?"

"Well, I know what Nilly would say about that, anyway," Lisa said. "'Give me liberty or give me death!'"

They all smiled at that thought. But then they all

felt even sadder. Then they thought a little more and a little more. Until Doctor Proctor finally said what they were all thinking: "There's nothing we can do."

Mrs Strobe emitted a little sob, bundled herself up in a wool blanket and disappeared into the living room, where she lay down on the sofa and flipped on the TV. They could hear her sneezing over the sounds of choral singing.

Lisa wanted to sob as well, but she put on her boots instead.

"I suppose maybe I ought to be getting home," she said. "True, my folks are hypnotised, but maybe they're worried about me anyway."

Doctor Proctor just nodded silently in response.

Lisa stepped out into the entryway, opened the front door and was just about to leave when she heard a familiar voice. She stopped immediately. The voice was coming from the living room.

"My fellow countrymen, it must be said sooner or

later: Happy New Year. But let me also add: Thank you for the old year. And now that that's out of the way, let me wish a speedy recovery to all who will fall ill this year. Especially the elderly, the lonely and all who are at sea. Together we are emerging from a noteworthy year here in Norway in which the chance of rain varied, national folk costumes were sewn, elk were hunted . . ."

Lisa felt a yawn sneaking up on her, but hurried back to the living room where Mrs Strobe was sitting in front of the TV, snoring. A guy in a red cloak with a white fur collar was staring out of the TV screen with a stiff expression as he droned on in a monotone: "But we have also seen a despot seize power and proclaim himself president."

"That's the king!" Lisa cried. "The king is giving his New Year's speech on TV!"

The Strobe Snore stopped suddenly, and Lisa heard the scrape of chair legs in the kitchen. And a second later, all three of them were sitting on the sofa, staring at the TV, their eyes wide.

"Hallvard Tenorsen's goal is not to create a better life for you, my fellow countrymen," the king said. "His goal is to create chaos and provide his baboons with breakfast. The truth is this: His real name is Yodolf Staler, and he is from the moon. He has hypnotised you through televised choral singing programmes, but there will be no more of that. For now we – my fellow countrymen, and all those who are at sea – are going to put a stop to Yodolf Staler. The Danes are our friends, and I urge you to lay down your arms immediately . . . Or as a matter of fact, you should instead turn your weapons on Yodolf Staler and his companions. And especially Butler Åke, that base, treasonous sneak of a butler."

"Excellent!" Doctor Proctor whispered. "He's doing it! It's just so . . . so . . ."

"It's the king. He's just doing his thing," Lisa said,

rolling her eyes a little to suggest that the king's New Year's address was rarely thrilling.

"But . . . but, was it in time?" whispered Mrs Strobe, anxiously. "Are we going to have time to save Gregory and Nilly? There's only a few hours until dawn . . ."

"I've got it!" Lisa said.

"What have you got?" Doctor Proctor asked.

"Marching-band music. The answer is marching-band music."

"Really?" Mrs Strobe asked.

"Of course," Lisa said. "We just have to drum up a band. Can you guys play anything? It doesn't matter what! Quick!"

"I can play a little piano," Mrs Strobe said. "I used to, anyway."

"Uh . . ." Doctor Proctor said, "I can play Frère Jacques on the recorder."

"We need more musicians," Lisa said. "We need

to hit the streets and recruit. And then we need a conductor . . . We need . . ."

MR MADSEN WOKE with a start. His doorbell was ringing. He discovered that he had fallen asleep in his recliner, and the TV was just playing static. The last thing he remembered before he fell asleep was choral singing. "Norway is good, Norway is best." Something like that. Very catchy, actually. Mr Madsen stuffed his feet into his slippers, buttoned up his marching-band-uniform jacket and shuffled over to open the door to his apartment.

There were three people out in the hallway. A girl who was puffing, a panting man in swim goggles, and a wheezing woman with an astoundingly long nose.

"We have to form a band," the girl said. "And we need to practise a song before the sun comes up!"

Mr Madsen adjusted his aviator sunglasses and stared at them blankly: "Do I know you?"

"I'm Lisa."

"Lisa?"

"I play in your band!"

"Band?" Mr Madsen thought for a second and then said, "Ugh, marshing band music is boring."

The girl sighed and turned to the woman with the purse. "He's hypnotised. Can you . . . ?"

The woman nodded, raised her hand and slapped it against the door. The smack was so loud that it reverberated down the stairwell. Mr Madsen blinked in confusion and saw Lisa, that professor chap, and Mrs Strobe, the teacher from his school, standing before him.

"Wh-where am I?" He turned and gazed into his apartment. On the floor there was a smashed flower vase, and the vertical hold on the TV needed to be adjusted.

"Say 'cheese,'" Lisa said.

"Cheese," Mr Madsen said. "What's going on?"

"You've been unhypnotised," Lisa said, grabbing her band director by the hand and pulling him along. "And now you're going to help us ring every doorbell on Cannon Avenue!"

DOCTOR PROCTOR WAS standing on a pear crate looking out over the crowd assembled in the glow of the streetlight right in the middle of Cannon Avenue. Everyone was there: commandant Mama, commandant Papa, Nilly's mother and sister and Mrs Thrane with Trym and Truls. Some of them were only wearing dressing gowns and pajamas, others were wearing thick down-filled parkas, some were in choral performance robes and some were in uniforms with rifles, more than ready to shoot themselves some Danes. But they had all heard the king's speech, and now they had just listened to Doctor Proctor, who filled them in on what was going on. Whether or not they believed him was another matter. The expressionless faces before him didn't give anything away.

"We need to start a rebellion," the professor said. "And we need to rescue Gregory and Nilly."

"Why?" someone in the crowd shouted. "Why should we risk our good health and our lives for a dwarf and a frog?"

"Because it's the right thing to do," Doctor Proctor said, sounding a little stronger now. "And because we *can*."

"Really?" someone else yelled, sounding skeptical. "So what's your plan, then?"

Doctor Proctor swallowed. "The plan, my dear friends . . . the plan is . . . now I'm sure you're eager to hear it . . ." He flashed his teeth in an awkward grin. "Which is quite reasonable of course, because it's a good plan . . . a brilliant plan . . . a plan that makes all other plans sound rather poorly planned out in comparison. It's the mother of all plans if you, uh . . . heh, heh . . . know what I mean . . ."

"No. What do you
mean?"

"The plan I'm talking about
is the very plan we have
planned to implement
in order to liberate no
less than Gregory and
Nilly. Isn't that a good
plan, don't you think?"

It was so quiet that you
could've heard a pin fall in the
snow. Until a shout pierced
the silence:

"What exactly is the
plan, you scarecrow?"

Doctor Proctor smiled quickly. "One second, techni-
cal difficulties." He leaned over to Lisa: "What's the
plan again?"

"To drum up a band and practise a song."

"A heck of a plan," Doctor Proctor said, straightening back up, taking a deep breath and shouting, "THE PLAN, LADIES AND GENTLEMEN . . ." before suddenly pausing to lean down to Lisa again.

"Which song and why?"

"Just tell them what I said."

Doctor Proctor straightened up again and said, "IS TO DRUM UP A BAND AND PRACTISE A SONG!"

For a second the crowd looked stunned. Then a roar of laughter erupted. Mr Madsen cleared his throat several times and adjusted his glasses. "Now now, people. This is serious business. *I* will be conducting."

"Who's General Numskull in that weird military uniform?" someone hollered.

"Is he blind?" a boy asked his father.

More laughter.

"Oh my God, what kind of song are you talking about?" Nilly's mother yelled.

"What kind of song?" Doctor Proctor repeated softly.

"A pop song," Lisa said, looking over to the east. Was the sky already starting to get lighter there at the bottom of the black edge of night?

"A POP SONG!" Doctor Proctor announced to the crowd. Which responded with the loudest wave of laughter of the day so far. Mrs Thrane, who was standing at the very front, with tears of laughter in her eyes, managed to choke out, "You're just crazy. You don't really mean to say in all seriousness that a *pop song* can save the world?"

"Who's with us?" Doctor Proctor cried.

Lisa looked out over the crowd, but to her dismay she saw only heads being shaken and could almost hear every single member of the crowd thinking, *I don't think so.* Then there was a small motion at the back of the crowd. Lisa could see now that two people were pushing their way through, towards the pear crate. One was carrying a big tuba, wearing patches over both eyeglass lenses, and was easy to recognise: It was Janne, the tuba player from band. But the other one was a pale girl with a frightened look on her face, which was just visible under the tufts of hair sticking up after what just might have been one of the worst haircuts of all time.

"Beatrize?" Lisa gasped in disbelief. She only just barely recognised the stooped girl, who didn't look anything like the cutest girl in the class as she stood there in the snowy street. "What happened to you?"

Beatrize's voice was just a whisper: "When the other girls got unhypnotised by the king's speech, they came over to my house. They said I had tricked them into joining the Norway Youth. Then they yanked me out onto the street and did this." She pointed at her head.

"That's terrible. Poor you!" Lisa said, appalled.

"I'm sorry for all the dumb, mean things I did."

Beatrize sniffled, her eyes full of tears: "C-c-can I join the band again? Please?"

Lisa glanced over at Mr Madsen, who nodded imperceptibly in response.

"Anyone who wants to," Lisa said, "can be in this band. Do you understand, Beatrize?"

Beatrize gulped, stared at the ground and nodded that she understood. Lisa put her hand on the shoulder of the former cutest girl in class. "Did you bring your saxophone?"

Beatrize looked up, smiled through her tears and held up her instrument case.

"Hey!" someone in the crowd shouted. "You haven't answered the question! A pop song can't save the world, can it?"

Lisa looked at Doctor Proctor, Mrs Strobe, and Mr Madsen. Then all four of them turned to face the crowd and replied in unison:

"Yes it can!"

Waffle Batter and the Songs of Migratory Birds

THERE WAS NO longer any doubt. Day was dawning. And when the sun rose, it was as if it was curious to see what was going on in this little big city. So it peeked up over the horizon and saw that something was happening in the rear courtyard in the middle of the snow-covered Royal Park that surrounded the palace. So the sun climbed higher into the sky to see. And from there it shone right onto a teeny tiny freckled face — wouldn't you know it? He was standing in the Royal Palace's rear courtyard, and next to him was a pale, greenish, grimacing face. Soldiers were arranged around them, and right in front of them stood an enormous shiny machine that the sun — if it hadn't known better — would have thought was an enormous behemoth of a waffle iron. And the sun hummed along to the song rising from the palace's rear courtyard on this morning: *"Honeydew — You are the melon, I dream of you . . ."*

NILLY FELT THE warmth on his face from the sun's rays, which had just peeked over the edge of the stone wall.

"Seems like spring is coming early this year," he said, closing his eyes.

"Yeah. It would just be so typical if this summer

turned out to be a really nice one, too," Gregory sniffled, yanking at the handcuffs that held his arms behind his back.

Nilly felt a wave of heat hit his face. "Ah, the sunshine feels so good," he said, without opening his eyes.

"That heat isn't coming from the sun," Gregory said softly.

Nilly opened his eyes. And from where he stood, on a chair, he was looking straight down into the black mouth of the waffle iron, which had just been opened. It sizzled with glistening grease flowing between the enormous steel teeth.

"Don't be scared," a voice behind them said. They turned. Yodolf Staler had camouflaged himself as Hallvard Tenorsen and was wearing a green uniform and a cap with a visor that had a red band around it. "There are international rules for the treatment of prisoners of war. And in them it says that waffle irons can only be used for cooking waffles. And I – Yodolf Staler –

am a man who follows rules. Which is why you will not be just tossed into the waffle iron any old which way . . ."

A sigh of relief could be heard coming from the soldiers. And a tremulous voice that whispered, "Thank God . . ."

"Who said that?" Yodolf growled, spinning around. The soldiers leaped to attention, staring straight ahead without moving so much as a nose hair.

"Is there someone here who wishes to object?" screamed Yodolf.

No response.

"What was that?" Yodolf bellowed.

The soldiers glanced at each other uncertainly, and a couple of them tentatively shook their heads. And then a few more. And finally they were all shaking their heads so eagerly that you could hear the brushing sound of hundreds of crew cuts rubbing against the insides of hundreds of uniform collars.

Yodolf eyed his soldiers with suspicion before turning back to Nilly and Gregory. "Where was I?"

"We're not going to be made into waffles . . ." Nilly said, concentrating on not losing his balance on the flimsy, unstable chair.

"I didn't say that," Yodolf said. "I said that you wouldn't be tossed into the waffle iron any old which way, since the rules say that waffle irons can only be used for making waffles. So . . . Göran!"

A soldier behind Yodolf stepped forwards. He was holding a fire hose. And Göran had been a little sloppy with his camouflage, because Nilly could see his hairy baboon hands sticking out of his soldier's uniform. Nilly followed the hose with his eyes, back to where it disappeared into a tent that was standing in one corner of the courtyard and serving as a field kitchen.

"So we'll make you into waffles first," Yodolf said. "Proceed, Göran!"

And in a soldierlike fashion, Göran turned on the fire

hose, which immediately started spraying something thick and yellow. The cascade hit Gregory so hard that he jumped back two steps.

When Gregory was covered in the yellow, dripping fluid, it was Nilly's turn. Nilly closed his eyes and stuck out his tongue when the liquid hit him. It tasted like waffle batter.

"Now you'll taste even better," Yodolf laughed. "Could I get two volunteer soldiers to toss them into the waffle iron?"

Göran responded, "Yes, yes! Pain! I want——"

"Not you, Göran. One of the human soldiers." Yodolf stared at the soldiers. But none of them moved. It was so quiet that the only thing that could be heard was the music: *"Honeydew – Knowing that breakfast will be with you . . ."*

"Okay," Yodolf said. "Then you and I will do it, Göran. Turn and face the waffle iron, prisoners."

Nilly turned, blinking waffle batter out of his eyes.

Then a songbird landed in a tree above the red-hot, smoking waffle iron and started singing. *I guess it came home a little too early,* Nilly thought, looking around at all the snow. But it was sitting there in the top of the pear tree, singing about spring coming a little early and combining with Agnes's voice.

"I hope they eat me with strawberry jam and whipped cream," Nilly whispered. "What do you want them to put on you? Maple syrup?"

"Doesn't matter," Gregory said. "Only a few days ago I wouldn't have thought it was so bad, being cooked and eaten. My life was so sad anyway. But now that I know that Mrs Strobe is out there, and maybe thinking about me, and maybe worrying about me . . ."

"Yeah," Nilly sighed, hearing Göran's footsteps approaching over the gravel. And it was like his fear about what was going to happen sharpened his senses, because he could hear more. The hum of a distant engine. And far away, a third song mixing with Agnes's

and the bird's. Then he felt Göran's eager breath on the back of his neck and the baboon claws against his back, and he felt himself being shoved forward towards the edge of the chair. Nilly closed his eyes and thought his last thought: that he hoped Lisa would be okay. He prepared himself.

"Wait!" Yodolf cried. "Take off their handcuffs."

"But . . ."

"If we're chewing them and we bite into the hand-cuffs, we might break a molar and then we'd have to go to the dentist and you know how I hate the dentist."

And as Nilly heard Göran fishing through his pockets for the keys to the handcuffs, swearing the whole time, he also heard the sound of the engine growing stronger. And the same went for the third song.

"Ah, there it is," Göran said, and Nilly heard the key turn first in his handcuffs and then in Gregory's. Then he heard Yodolf's wicked laughter.

"And now, darn it, now they'll be some filthy britches."

A Pop Song
Saves the World.
Maybe.

ONE OF THE two guards at the palace's front gate shielded his eyes and squinted into the low morning sunlight, in the direction the engine sound was coming from.

"Say, Gunnar," he said, tugging on his handlebar mustache. "Isn't that an awfully large motorcycle?"

"The biggest I've ever seen, Rolf," the other guard said, raising his upper lip and sniffing his own Fu Manchu mustache. "Sort of looks like it's pulling along a whole theatre seating box. With, what's that in it? A brass band?"

"What's that they're playing? Sounds familiar . . ."

"Wait! They're turning. They're coming up here! Look, they're coming! What's going on?"

"Something's going to happen!"

"Listen! They're playing . . . they're playing . . ."

"She luvs ya, nah, nah, nah?"

"DRIVE RIGHT IN the front gate, Professor!" Lisa shouted from the sidecar.

"Will do," called Doctor Proctor, who was leaning in over the motorcycle's handlebars, giving it gas as they approached Palace Square. "Just play as loud as you can!"

"Did you hear that?" Mr Madsen yelled from the

sidecar, and started swinging his baton in even larger arcs. And the strangest band that ever played in a sidecar didn't need any urging. Lisa was playing the clarinet, Mrs Strobe was hammering on the keys of a toy piano, Janne was on the tuba, Beatrize was playing the saxophone, Lisa's commandant father was rocking out on a guitar with two broken strings, Lisa's commandant mother was playing a piccolo, Trym and Truls were on the snare drums and Nilly's sister was swinging a mallet against a base drum, while Nilly's mother screamed so piercingly off-key, unappealingly and loudly that the tourists in Palace Square gaped and covered their ears, "She luvs ya, nah, nah, nah! She luvs ya, nah, nah, nah!"

The two guards snapped to attention, one on the left, one on the right, as the motorcycle drove through the gate onto Palace Square.

* * *

NILLY HEARD THE music, heard De Beetels' "She luvs ya, nah, nah, nah" drowning out BABA's "Honeydew," heard Agnes's voice being drowned out by the kitchen-sink-style spectacle from Doctor Proctor's sidecar band. Nilly knew it was his friends coming to save him. But what help could they be? It was too late. Göran had already given him the push, and Nilly fell, off the chair and down into the waffle iron's searing heat.

He saw his life flash before his eyes. There had been highs and lows, lots of fun, a couple of days that could've been better, but most of all there had been jelly, fart powder and adventures with good friends. The short summary: a life that was way too short for a guy who was way too short. But now it was over.

Slorp!

What was that?

There was suddenly a blue belt around Nilly's stomach. And he wasn't falling anymore. Or rather he was falling . . . up. Or the opposite of falling – he was

rising. He saw the exterior wall of the palace rushing past and – *plop!* – he landed. The blue belt, which wasn't a belt at all but a blue frog tongue, loosened its hold, and Nilly saw that he was back on the same balcony he'd been standing on a few days before. Gregory was standing next to him, spitting.

"You jumped up here?!" Nilly exclaimed, peering down at the courtyard below, where the motorcycle was driving around the waffle iron pursued by Göran and Yodolf and Tandoora. "With me in your tongue?!"

"Blech!" Gregory said. "You taste like grass and soap."

"You saved me!" Nilly said, throwing his arms around Gregory.

"Hey, not so fast!" Gregory said, flailing his arms in an attempt to get Nilly off him. "I'm not sure we're safe yet."

And he was absolutely right about that, because the motorcycle was now surrounded by soldiers, and suddenly someone turned the BABA music way up.

It was so loud that Cannon Avenue's sidecar band was totally drowned out by the sound of Agnes: *"HONEYDEW – FINALLY SLICING MY HONEYDEW!!"*

And Nilly saw Gregory grow pale again, saw his knees start shaking, saw him slowly buckle. Until Agnes took a breath after *DEW*, and in that gap, a desperate cry was heard from the courtyard:

"Gregory! I love you!"

"Hiccup!" Gregory said. "What was that?"

"That," Nilly replied, "was someone saying they love you."

"Love m-m-me? But wh-who . . ."

"Who do you think, frog brain? Mrs Strobe, of course! Duh!"

And Nilly saw a healthy green colour flood back through Gregory's cheeks. His eyes started to twinkle, and a large smile spread across his face.

"We have to do something before the soldiers get them!" Nilly said.

But Gregory didn't seem to hear Nilly; he was staring off into space with a blissful look on his face. "This is actually a pretty good song, isn't it?" he said.

"Honeydew?" Nilly asked, taken aback.

"Yeah, when you *really* listen to it," Gregory said.

"Hello? Earth to Gregory! Wake up!" Nilly said, snapping his fingers just in front of Gregory's face. "Uh, the end of the world and all that?"

And then there was a *swish!* A *slorp!* A *swoosh!* A *smack!* And an *eeeek!*

The *smack!* was the sound of the three soldiers — after Gregory's tongue picked them up and flung them away — hitting the wall of the building. And the *eeeek!* was the sound of the one of those three who had the misfortune to hit the top of a picture window and was now slowly sliding down.

Yodolf was jumping up and down and trying to issue orders to the soldiers: "Shoot them! Stop that god-awful clanking toy orchestra! Shoot them all!"

Some of the soldiers hesitantly raised their weapons and aimed at the sidecar, but they didn't fire.

"Now! This is a presidential order! And anyone who doesn't obey will have to face a court martial and treason charges and season charges and bleazon charges . . . and . . . and . . . JUST SHOOT!"

But no one shot.

"My dear Norwegians!" Nilly yelled from the balcony, and the soldiers turned and gazed up at him in surprise. "Now is the time for us to show that we won't let ourselves be ordered around by baboons and bandits and brutal bullies!"

"Shooooot the traitor!" Yodolf screamed, pointing a trembling black index-finger fingernail at the balcony.

"I can't promise you that it will be easy," Nilly said in a thunderous voice. "Quite the contrary, all I can promise is stinky feet! But . . ." He raised his hand in a majestic gesture. "I can promise you this: No more choral singing on TV! So the question is: What do you pick? Brass instruments or choral singing?"

"Shoot!" Yodolf sobbed, and then went suddenly quiet as he heard the trigger mechanism click and discovered that the weapons were finally being aimed – at him.

"Waaaaa," Yodolf said. And that very instant he disappeared. Vanished. Into thin air.

"He camouflaged himself!" Nilly yelled. "Quick, don't let him get away. Guards, shut the gate!"

"Did you hear what he said, Gunnar?" Handlebar said to Fu Manchu. They were standing at the gate and had been following all the commotion in the courtyard with their eyes agog.

"Yup, Rolf. He said we should shut the gate."

"That's what I thought. And you know what, Gunnar?"

"No, what Rolf?"

"I think it's time for real Norwegians to switch sides."

"Yeah, it does seem like the tide has turned. We

ought to turn with it, Rolf. Then we'll be heroes of the resistance, little old us!"

"Quick thinking, Gunnar, quick thinking."

And with that they shut the massive iron gate. And the second it clicked shut and locked, they heard a smacking sound, as if someone had run into the gate, followed by a horrendously ugly Swedish swearword that we won't repeat here.

IN THE COURTYARD, Doctor Proctor had stopped the motorcycle, and as the Cannon Avenue brass band continued to play, Mrs Strobe leaped out and disappeared into the kitchen tent. And she must have located the device that was playing "Honeydew" in there, because Lisa heard Mrs Strobe shout "Aha!" followed by the sound of a desk slap, and there won't be any more BABA music heard during the rest of this story.

The soldiers were running around in the courtyard,

fumbling, searching for moon chameleons, who had all made themselves invisible by now. Suddenly Doctor Proctor fell off the motorcycle, and someone tried to start it up. But Lisa's commandant father swung his guitar as hard as he could down onto the driver's seat where it struck something – even though it looked like there was just air there – and the centre of the guitar splintered with a crunching sound.

"I've got one of them!" Lisa's commandant father yelled, holding on tight to the neck of the guitar.

A desperate female voice wailed from inside the guitar, "Yodolf! Don't let them take us! Save me! Yodolf! Yodolf, you big letdown! Yodo—"

Tandoora didn't have a chance to say anything else before she was tackled by soldiers and someone snapped the same handcuffs onto her that Gregory Galvanius had been wearing.

In a snowdrift over in the corner of the courtyard, two of the soldiers had got hold of something, but both got bopped in the nose and fell over backwards.

"Welcome to a world of hurt, you idiotic creep!" Göran screamed. "Come to Daddy now! Come — umph!"

The *umph* sound was because Göran had just been struck by something big and heavy that came from above, which shoved him down into the snow.

"Umph!"

The second *umph* sound was because Göran was struck a second time by something big and heavy that came from above and pushed him even a little deeper into the snow.

"Double umph!"

The third *umph* sound . . . well, you've probably figured it out.

And when Göran, now several feet deep in the snow, gasped and looked up, he saw something way up above him in the air, a frog man in midjump, on his way down. *Filthy britches,* he thought, closing his eyes.

* * *

BUT WHERE WAS Yodolf?

Lisa had set down her clarinet and was standing in the sidecar, surveying the chaos in the courtyard, but there was no Yodolf Staler to be seen.

Doctor Proctor came over to her and said exactly what she was thinking: "If Staler gets away, he'll be back. Maybe with an even more dastardly plan."

Lisa looked around at the stone walls surrounding the courtyard. They were tall, but a desperate baboon could probably make it over them. There was no time to waste. She jumped out of the sidecar and ran over to the fire hose, picked it up and released the lever that was stopping the flow.

"What are you doing?" Doctor Proctor asked, staring at the lumpy yellow waffle batter that the fire hose started splurting out.

"I'm going to find Yodolf," Lisa said, pulling on the lever and aiming the hose straight up.

The yellow jet grew more vigorous and travelled up towards the blue morning sky and the sun that was shining with dismay on the bizarre things the people and animals of Oslo were up to. When the waffle batter decided it had gone high enough, it turned and came splattering back down again. It coated the ice-covered cobblestones, balconies, uniform hats, freckled nose tips, jumping frog men and scrambling soldiers. But most important of all: It coated a form that until now had been invisible.

"Thewe he is!" cried a waffle-battered shape that was suspiciously reminiscent of Mrs Strobe.

And sure enough, in the middle of the courtyard they saw a waffle-batter-dripping silhouette, shaped like a baboon. It was bending over the same manhole cover that Nilly and Gregory had climbed out of several days earlier. And just as the soldiers were storming over to the waffle baboon, it got the cover up, jumped down into the hole and was gone.

Nilly slid down from the roof on the downspout and came running over to Lisa and Doctor Proctor, who were already standing next to the hole peering down.

"It'll be catastrophic if he gets away," Doctor Proctor said.

"I know," Nilly said, and then mumbled, "And it would be extraordinarily good luck if someone here happened to have a flashlight on them, wouldn't it?"

All of the soldiers standing around them started fishing around in their uniforms, and a second later twenty-four torches were being held out to Nilly.

"Standard-issue field equipment, Sergeant," one of them explained.

"As you were," Nilly said, grabbing one of the torches and pinching his nose between his thumb and index finger: "Who's coming?"

"I am," the professor said, checking that his swimming goggles were on securely and pinching his nose as well.

"And me!" called Gregory, who had stopped jumping

up and down on Göran and was instead over by the kitchen tent eating waffle batter off the face of a waffle-batter-covered form that bore a suspicious resemblance to Mrs Strobe.

Lisa groaned, pinched her own nose and said in a nasal voice, "Why do we ALWAYS end up down the stinking sewers?"

"How else would we be able to . . ." Nilly began.

"Get out of them again?" Lisa sighed and jumped. And presto! She was gone. And presto! Nilly was gone. And two prestos later, the professor and Gregory were right behind them.

"WELL, THIS IS quite dark," Doctor Proctor said, once they'd all landed with some large and some not quite so large splashes in the sewer water.

"Oh, and it reeks!" said Lisa in disgust, trying to wring out her hair.

"But at least it washed the waffle batter off us,"

Nilly said, switching on the flashlight.

"That's just it," Doctor Proctor said. "How will we find Yodolf if all the waffle batter has washed off?"

"We don't even know if we should start heading right or left," Lisa said.

Three of the four friends looked at each other, perplexed.

The fourth, Gregory, started hiccuping.

"Hiccup!" he said. *"Hicketty hick!"*

"There, there," Doctor Proctor soothed. "This is no time to get all stressed out, Gregory."

"He's just asking which way Yodolf went," Nilly explained.

"Asking who?"

Nilly swung his torch around. It landed on a pair of shiny frog eyes.

"Hiccup," the frog said. *"Hic-hiccup!"*

"This way," Gregory said, pointing, and Nilly waded down the pipe with the beam of light ahead of him.

The others followed, Doctor Proctor bending over so that he wouldn't hit his head on the top of the pipe. Suddenly Nilly stopped. They were at a crossroads where the one pipe split into five different pipes.

"Hiccup!" Gregory said. *"Hicketty hick!"*

And a brief croak came from the darkness in response.

"Ugh," Gregory said.

"What?" Lisa asked.

"They didn't see anyone go by here."

"Well that's that, then," Doctor Proctor said. "Yodolf must have washed the rest of the batter off and now he's camouflaging himself again. We'll never find him."

And the others realised that the professor was right.

"Bummer," Lisa said. "I was so hoping that this would have a really good ending, with Yodolf safely under lock and key."

"We'll have to make do with a fairly good ending," Doctor Proctor said. "And hope that Yodolf Staler doesn't show up again anytime soon."

They nodded to each other.

"Let's go back," Doctor Proctor said.

"Hiccup."

Three of the four friends started wading back the same way they'd come.

"Nilly!" Lisa yelled. "Aren't you coming?"

She turned around and looked at her little friend, who was standing there staring into the darkness.

"What is it, Nilly?"

"That last hiccup," he said. "It sounded familiar."

"I'm sure all frog croaks sound kind of the same," Lisa said.

"That was no frog," Nilly said, aiming the flashlight into the darkness in one of the tunnels. "It was . . . it was . . . !" he cried out in joy.

And the others saw him hold out his hand, but couldn't tell what for. But then they understood.

"Perry!" Nilly cried. "Perry, you made it! Have you been down here this whole time?"

"Hiccup."

Lisa and the others turned around and came back to Nilly.

"Amazing!" Doctor Proctor laughed. "Now, my dear friends, despite everything, we have no choice but to be satisfied with the ending of this story!"

"Almost," Nilly said. "Shh!"

He cocked his head to the side, towards the little seven-legged Peruvian sucking spider that he had placed on his shoulder.

"Perry wants us to go this way," Nilly said, and started running down one of the tunnels. There was less water there, but what little there was splashed around his feet. The others hurried after him. And when they rounded a turn, they saw Nilly standing there, legs apart. And in front of him was a large, beautiful cobweb that stretched across the whole sewer tunnel, its strands glittering in the light.

"Look!" Nilly whispered.

And they looked. They saw that the cobweb was moving. As if something large and invisible were thrashing about helplessly in the network of threads that was so strong they must have been spun by a spider who had consumed Doctor Proctor's Strength Tonic with Mexican Thunder Chili, Maximum Strength. And when they looked more carefully, they could see that the shape still had splotches of waffle batter here and there.

Lisa positioned herself next to Nilly and reached out her hand. And shuddered when she felt it encounter something warm and hairy.

"Yodolf Staler," Nilly said in a deep voice. "So we were fated to meet again."

"Shut up, you dwarf!" a familiar, enraged voice screamed from inside the cobweb. "Let me out of here!"

"We'd be happy to," Doctor Proctor said. "We'll send a few nice soldiers down who'll put some nice, shiny handcuffs on you and give you a free lift to a snug, warm cage. And who knows? Maybe you'll get to be on display at the zoo. To strike a little fear into the hearts of visitors."

"Aaaargh!" came the snarl from the cobweb. And slowly he came into view. Yodolf Staler. Lisa shuddered again when she saw those sharp teeth gleaming in that open mouth.

And as they turned around to go back, Lisa hoped she would never see Yodolf Staler again, in a zoo or anywhere else. And she wouldn't, either.

But from then on, Lisa stopped thinking about all that stuff. Because when our friends emerged into the daylight in the palace's rear courtyard, the festivities were already in full swing. The soldiers were dancing around and people were gathered outside the gate waving small Norwegian flags and shouting, "Hurrah!"

"Party!" Nilly shouted, doing the moonwalk into the middle of the crowd. "Bring on the girls, jelly, and song!"

And that's exactly what happened.

30

An Animal You Wish Didn't Exist. Except Right Now.

"WELL, THIS IS certainly fun, Rolf," Gunnar said, snapping the handcuffs around the hairy wrists of Yodolf, who was dangling from the ceiling of the tunnel, swaddled in cobwebs, down in the sewers. They had put a piece of tape over Yodolf's mouth after they got tired of listening to him promise them first money, then gold and even green forestland if they would let him escape, and then – after they politely declined his offers – he threatened to bite off their stupid heads with those stupid hats if they didn't let him go immediately. Now the baboon couldn't make a sound, and it was so quiet Rolf and Gunnar could hear the music and cheering from the people aboveground. The celebration had spread to include all of Oslo, yes, even all of Norway, where people were now pouring out onto the streets to celebrate and congratulate each other on being free from Staler the despot.

Rolf wiped his cheek where one of the girls in Palace Square had kissed him.

"Feels good doesn't it, Gunnar, to have liberated Norway?" He laughed.

"They'll write epic poems about us," Gunnar said, fastening cuffs around the unpleasant moon chameleon's ankles.

"They'll build a museum in our honour and make movies about our heroic deeds," Rolf said.

Gunnar tried to prize Yodolf free from the cobwebs. "I have to say, he's good and stuck in this web. Give me a hand here, Rolf, would you?"

"Of course, Gunnar."

But even together they couldn't get Yodolf free.

"It's like glue," Rolf groaned. "We're going to have to get some monster hedge clippers and clip him free."

"Good thinging."

"I think you meant 'thinking.'"

"I think you're probably right about that, Rolf."

They pulled the tape off Yodolf's mouth so he wouldn't suffocate while they were gone, and started wading back the same way they'd come while Yodolf screamed after them, "Numbskulls! Filthy britches!"

Suddenly Gunnar stopped.

"What is it?" Rolf asked.

"Did you see that?"

"What?"

"In the dark over there. A flash of white. Like teeth in an enormous jaw full of teeth."

"How enormous?"

"Well. Like an inflatable swim ring."

"Quit kidding around, Rolf."

"Uh, you're Rolf."

"Gunnar, I mean. You don't believe that old urban legend that's going around, about an anaconda living in the sewers under Oslo, the one that's supposed to be eighteen yards of solid, constrictor muscles with teeth like upside-down ice cream cones. I'm sorry, but if you believe that one, well then you're more gullible than . . ."

He was interrupted by a loud shriek and an even louder bang.

"What was that sound?"

"If I didn't know better, I'd say it was an enormous jaw suddenly snapping shut and someone making a cry for help."

"More like half a cry for help."

"Yeah. 'Hel—!' That was it."

"Yeah. 'Hel—!' And then it stopped."

"As if the cry was cut in half."

"Hm. Do you hear anything else?"

"No."

"Exactly. He's awfully quiet all of a sudden."

"You mean . . ."

They turned around slowly and shone their torches at the cobweb. And there, in the middle of the cobweb, where a thrashing, writhing, furious moon chameleon had been hanging just a few seconds before, now there wasn't one. Not even a cobweb. As if someone had taken a big bite. A bite the size of . . . well, an inflatable swim ring.

"R-R-Rolf?" Gunnar asked as they backed away, shining the light everywhere. "D-d-do you think anacondas like moon chameleons?"

"I – I – I don't know, Gunnar. I wouldn't think so.

But maybe if they had a little bit of a waffle taste?"

And with that they both spun around and ran as fast as they could out of the sewer and up into the daylight. And there they stood, blinking in the sunshine, surrounded by people dancing, balloons flying, fireworks exploding and flags waving. And then girls stepped over and kissed both of them on both cheeks – the cheeks with the handlebar mustache and the cheeks with the Fu Manchu mustache – and they joined right in with the dancing and forgot all about Yodolf and at least half about the anaconda.

Girls, jelly and Song

THE NEXT AFTERNOON there was a party at the crooked blue house at the top of Cannon Avenue. And since the sun was shining even more enthusiastically than the day before, Doctor Proctor, Lisa and Nilly had brought dining-table chairs, the holey sofa and the barbecue out into the garden. The entire thrown-together-at-the-last-minute Cannon Avenue band plus neighbours and friends were there. The melting snow gurgled and laughed in the gutters and storm drains as the guests ate their grilled hot dogs. And these weren't just any old grilled hot dogs; they were South Trøndelag grilled hot dogs, brought to the party by a special guest who had landed his hang glider in the garden earlier that day. And who was now playing Chinese checkers with another special guest.

"I do believe, Your Royal Highness," Petter said with his mouth full of hot dog, moving the last blue and yellow marble into place, "that I just won."

The king looked down at the game board and mumbled, "Well, I'll be!"

Petter tipped his head back and yelled at the blue sky, "Fight, Petter! So wonderful, Petter! Three cheers for Petter! I'm the one and only Petter . . ."

And then Nilly tapped on his glass with a knife to let everyone know he was going to say something. Silence settled over the snow-covered yard. Nilly leaped up onto his chair and cleared his throat:

"People are strange," he began. "When we feel like strangling someone, it's usually one of the people we love the most."

"Yup!" Nilly's sister called out.

"We elected Yodolf as president," Nilly continued. "But it is very human to be fooled and to make mistakes. Yes indeed, even I readily admit that I myself have been wrong on two occasions."

Lisa, who was sitting next to Nilly, elbowed him in the side. Nilly cleared his throat again:

"Maybe even three times. But what's important is that you're brave enough to admit that you made a mistake. In fact, people really *ought* to make mistakes sometimes. Because how else would you ever get the chance to correct your mistakes?"

Nilly paused to give everyone a chance to mull this over. Then he continued:

"We are here today to celebrate the fact that we fought for something. But what did we actually fight for? The right to be little and know how to spell? Is that important enough to risk wafflisation for?"

He looked around.

"Yes," Lisa said, standing up too. "Because it's not just about the right to be little or good at spelling. It's just as much about the right to be big and be bad at spelling. It's about the right to be both the same and different."

Lisa and Nilly bowed and sat back down. Applause broke out and Lisa gave her commandant father and commandant mother a stern look so they would understand it was embarrassing that they kept clapping for so long after everyone else had stopped.

"That girl's going to be prime minister one day," the king whispered to Gregory and Mrs Strobe. Then he tapped his knife on his glass and jumped up:

"My fellow countrymen, I too would like to say

something. It has been an eventful year, and there is more to come."

Nilly's mother yawned so loudly that her jaws made a popping sound.

"But most of all I would like to make a proclamation," the king said. "Two of the people here today have decided to get engaged. And I'm so proud because they asked if I would be the best man. Ladies and gentlemen, I present to you . . . Rosemarie Strobe and Gregory Galvanius."

Cheers rose through the air, and a smiling, red-cheeked Mrs Strobe raised her glass for a toast. Then Gregory put his arms around her and asked her loudly if he could have a kiss.

Everyone cheered and Nilly raised his glass of pear juice. "Then with that I declare the war over. Let dessert begin. Because as fate would have it, Doctor Proctor and his fiancée Juliette, who returned home from Paris today, have made jelly."

A long, expectant "ooooh" ran through the crowd and everyone turned towards the blue house, from which the professor and his fiancée had just emerged. Over their heads, their arms straight, they were holding the longest tray anyone had ever seen.

"Th-th-that's a gigantic jelly – that must weigh as mush as a house!"

At the sound of 'mush,' it was like everyone in the yard suddenly froze. Everyone stared in horror at the man who'd said it.

"Uh, heh heh," Mr Madsen laughed, embarrassed and self-conscious, and then adjusted his sunglasses. "Just kidding."

And cheers broke out again.

AND WE LEAVE our friends there. We take a hang glider, perhaps, and fly up into the air. Over the garden with that blue house, where they're still shovelling the longest jelly anyone has ever eaten into their mouths.

Over the pear tree where a bird is singing about a slightly too early spring. Over the city of Oslo, where people are still dancing in the streets and the sun is shining on everyone. And we follow one of the rays of sunlight, the one that shines down on a manhole cover, through a little hole and on down into Oslo's jungle of sewer pipes and tunnels. We can maybe hear something smacking its lips down there in the darkness. Full and content. I know what you're thinking, but you don't actually believe those old stories. Do you?